THE

Production by eBookPro Publishing
www.ebook-pro.com

THE HIDDEN HOUSE IN TENERIFE
Shay Porat
Copyright © 2024 Shay Porat

All rights reserved; no parts of this book may be reproduced
or transmitted in any form or by any means, electronic
or mechanical, including photocopying, recording, taping,
or by any information retrieval system, without
the permission, in writing, of the author.

Translation from Hebrew: Julia Ehrenfeld
Editing: Nancy Alroy

Contact: shay@shayporat.com
www.shayporat.com

ISBN 9798301607691

The Hidden House in Tenerife

A Novel

SHAY PORAT

*Though I did go on a trip to Tenerife,
this book is a figment of my imagination
and any connection to actual events,
places and people is purely coincidental.*

Chapter 1

I pack a small trolley bag. Three shirts, pants, some underwear and socks, toiletries, exhaustion and fatigue, cups overflowing with sorrow. I'm flying away from here.

It sounds so jaded and banal to say that every journey begins with one small step. For me, it starts when I get on the train to the airport. The three-foot metal rotating turnstiles with their flashing lights, the green-and-red barcode readers—are my small step.

I swipe my boarding pass on the scanner. Like a wheel turning to push me onto the first step—onto no longer being here.

I take the first seat in the first empty car I can find, and set my body on the blue upholstery. I try to rein in my impatience that is like an eager horse about to break out of the stable and gallop to the fields.

My cell phone rings.

"Hey, what's up?" I answer, trying to sound normal.

"Any feedback from the Troy Group?" I am used to this. To not being asked how I am. To no interest being shown in me personally, but rather getting straight down to business. It's part of who he is. With the people he loves, people he trusts and believes in, he wastes no time on chit-chat. My senior partner. Or actually, I am his junior partner.

"I haven't. They said it's between us and *Quash Media & Public Affairs.*"

I know what's going on right now. What was going on from the moment we first met, a decade ago when I considered switching from being a salaried executive to becoming a partner, albeit a minor one, in another firm. I was convinced that was what was missing in my life. I could not figure out how, despite making money, and good money at that, driving a cool car, having access to an open expense account and certainly no shortage of professional challenges—something still wasn't working out for me. I was irritable and unhappy.

Back to my partner who, by now, is most likely raising his hand in the air, shaking his wrist in rhythm to the to the cracking of the joint, airing the discomfort of where the metal strap of his Chopard watch touches his skin and making a slight clicking sound as it bounces. This is exactly what he always does when my answers don't fully satisfy him.

"I don't like it." This is who he is. Transparent and one hundred percent open with me. Saying everything point blank. I could almost guess what was coming next. "Give Lisa a call and find out what's going on and whether this requires some maneuver." I say the last sentence to myself along with him, word for word. Maneuver. That had to come from a man who served in an infantry brigade.

"Fine."

He hangs up.

As the train starts to move, a couple sits down not far from me, breaking the silence in the car.

"To be honest, the performance wasn't all that good." He is broad. He takes up a seat and then some. Something in him is blown up. I don't mean he's arrogant. On the contrary, he's even got some charm. I mean physically. He's a little swollen, like he's been stung by a bee or is suffering from the heat. He is also very tall and looks disheveled. A black coat thrown over a frayed earth-brown shirt whose hems flutter outside his pants. In general, it seems sloppiness is his way of life. Or at least at this point in his life.

"You have a point there. That's why I want to go watch the other show that's now in town." The answer comes from the seat opposite him. A thin pair of glasses with one-and-a-half-inch-diameter lenses delicately covering blue eyes, a freckled face, black Renaissance curls and extremely gaunt. There is no sign of breasts.

"If he redeemed himself like that singer, that rapper who gave everyone who was at that concert free tickets— that would be really cool," the large man replies. His huge legs hardly fit under the table between the chairs. That's why he is constantly rearranging them. I glance sideways, trying to guess the size of his bright green sneakers. Fifteen? Maybe sixteen?

"I've got to be home by seven, but let's tell them instead that we're going to a live music show."

"Good. That's what we'll tell them," he says, as he pulls a record out of its cover. "By the way, when we get there, I intend to sell it to them for at least fifty euros."

"What do you mean 'fifty?' You need a hundred and fifty or maybe three hundred and fifty. That's the selling price. Let's agree on that."

"OK. I'll ask for more and explain to them that's the amount I've gotta have. I want to buy the new Prometheus record. By the way, they told me they were saving the pink album for me." His brown eyes open wide. His self-confident look leaves no room for doubt. "They're holding it for me."

The train clatters in tandem with its chugging, taking part in the conspiracy. It makes sure that just when an important sentence is voiced, exactly on the beat, the noise muffles the words. But I furrow my brow, casually tilting my head to a better angle to keep the information flowing.

The thin hand embeds the phone into a sea of black curls, deep towards the ear.

"Listen, Dad. About that concert downtown I texted about earlier? Jill is checking with the others in the squad. Her parents have a big car, she's got her license now and, if there are enough people, we will all drive there with her. It'll be over at half past eleven, the latest."

The big man leans back a little, waiting to see what curly hair's conversation yields. "Yes, of course, today." A momentary pause and then, "Thanks, Dad." She places the cell phone on the small table between them, her hands go up in a coordinated motion, and she pulls her elbows down to the sides of her body. "Yesss," she whistles, baring her teeth.

"Maybe I'll ask my mom too... I talked to her about it this morning and she said we'd have plenty of time to decide later."

The big man is probably thinking about what was just said, and replies, "The thing I like about you is that, once we decide to be practical, you never take your eyes off the goal." Meant as a compliment I suppose, but the complimentee is already deep into her next move.

"Mom, listen. First, I've already asked Dad, and he basically agrees. So here it goes. Today is the concert in the city." Pause. She takes a deep breath, filling her lungs with air, which makes her look like she just blew up to double her skinny size. The plain black shirt rises. Curly hair lifts her gaze for a moment by an inch or so, and then she says with complete confidence: "Mom, it's she, not he." She pauses for another second, exhales and continues: "Jill is now checking with everyone. It ends at eleven thirty. Like, the doors open at eight thirty or nine. She's already got her license, so she doesn't need supervision. Not even at night." After a few moments, a wide smile spreads across her face. "Thanks, Mom." She hangs up.

"It reassures her whenever I say I've already asked Dad. Even though they're divorced, if it's an out-of-town performance, they both need to agree."

"Makes sense," Big Guy agrees. "Even if they were still married, they'd surely consult with each other on a matter like this."

Then Big Guy, in turn, repeats the exact same speech to his mother. He reminds her that they had talked about it earlier, and she said they'd decide later as there was still time. So yeah, the time has come.

When I get back from the toilet, they're no longer there. I don't think about it too much. My phone is buzzing. It's a text message: *Danny from Shipman Industries is looking for you regarding the product with the malfunction. He asked that you contact them asap because the product is already on customer's premises.*

Chapter 2

"Stress is an automatic reflex of the nervous system. This reflex is activated every time you face the prospect of your birthday dinner in a complex family dynamic, or when your boss calls you in for a talk and you have no idea why. This mechanism becomes more acute, extreme and sensitive in those who have been through some traumatic, particularly shocking, life-changing event. You should consider managing your stress levels by using the Four A's: Avoid, Alter, Adapt, and Accept."

(From the Stress Management Guidebook)

The train's jolting overwhelms me again with an image of him holding his TravelPass card. The next jolt brings back that time I came to pick him up from the train station and caught a glimpse of him, out of the corner of my eye, hugging a girl goodbye, his back toward me and she clinging to him tightly with her eyes closed. The next one reminds me of the time we went to the zoo. On the way back, the train occasionally swayed left and right. Exhausted from a day full of excitement running around and watching the animals, he just rested his head on my lap. I feel the warmth of his body filling me once again.

I really can't be here any longer. Feeling like I'm derailing, I grab my carry-on bag. This makes going to the airport even more urgent, watching a plane take off through a transparent teardrop. As a disciplined, law-abiding citizen, I am addicted to the process itself. There's nothing like a well-lit place that's alive 24/7 to encourage obedience, is there?

Floodlights that are never turned off. A moderate rumble. The gods of volume—way up there. I am, of course, referring to the higher echelons of the aviation authorities. The gods that accurately set a steady murmur at a level of three or four out of ten, and no louder. Swarms of people who know their places, gearing themselves up for *Modern Times* à la Charlie Chaplin.

I set foot on the tiles of the life-sized pinball machine and picture the path I'll be following: find your flight on the departures board and launch yourself into the lanes leading to your airline's check-in counters. If you play well, you'll get the seat you wanted and meet your baggage again at the other end. A thin strip for the hand luggage security check feeding through the mouse hole rolls you over to passport control and, from there, to the duty free area. The hope of each such human ball is to arrive at the next part of its journey—into an airplane seat—after rolling into gate B9, I8 or I1 and transporting itself through the tunnel, only to be met by flight attendants who await them with a smile, sometimes a fake one, that hides the long day (or night) they've had or the pain in their legs, and who will direct them towards the seat. Oh, and let's not forget the pleasure of sipping an expensive and not-that-great-tasting cup of coffee that brands every traveler in a selfie to be broadcast on social networks so everyone knows you're going on a trip.

Dutifully I file into the Zone A line toting my blue carry-on bag behind me. At this point it is important for me to point out that a line is not what it seems. A line is a living organism. It isn't a group of people who just happened to gather because they are all about to embark on a flight with an airline departing from this open counter. Even without their knowledge, they have a common goal: to not be here, in the deepest sense of the term.

Take, for example, six feet ahead of me—a very tall woman in black heels wearing a well-tailored suit. Her hair is dyed blonde. Next to her stands someone who looks like a friend or a personal assistant who has become a sort of companion, at least until she gets fired.

"These things shouldn't happen. Approve it right away," the blonde yells with the Bluetooth buds deep inside her ear. She says it with the decisiveness reserved for a death sentence.

The friend, or assistant, immediately backs her up. "Excellent," she says, "and, by the way, those earrings flatter you." And then, "Where did you buy them?"

Just as she is about to answer, a young man interrupts them, asking in a piercing voice if she is also on the flight to Dubai, because it may be delayed due to the high traffic.

"We're on the flight to Madrid, which was probably delayed too. But don't worry, they won't take off without you. You're already in the line," replies the friend, or assistant, probably replying out of habit on behalf of her boss, the same way she probably sometimes signed documents with her name, so she wouldn't have to be bothered conversing with a stranger.

"The flight to Madrid has a two-hour delay," interjects a young woman from the other end of the line, a full ten people ahead of me. "It's a serious fuck up," she says. Oddly enough, even when she says 'fuck' her face lights up, as if she's found the formula for happiness. "I'll probably miss my connection to Casablanca and, from there, the train to Marrakech." Only now do I notice her huge backpack, much bigger than she is.

"Why would you miss it? How much time do you have between landing and the next flight?"

Actually, I'm also on the flight to Madrid. Though I have nothing to add to the conversation, I really want to intervene. Maybe to kill some time. So I make it up as I go along.

"Two and a half hours." She turns her head to me and, as she says this, I feel the little ray of sunshine above her. She volunteers, without anyone asking her, that she has already had connecting flights at least ten times over the past two years. The last time was a week ago. She is a *mochilera*. Travel now. Life decisions afterwards.

"Well, I try to leave at least five to eight hours for my connections, just for cases like these." I try but fail to get a conversation going beyond that.

A little further from us stands a quiet man. The laces of both his high work boots are partially undone. His jeans fit loosely on his waist. He has thick glasses with brown rims. He seems to be completely outside the line. Sometimes he even seems to be in a haze while others overtake him, until someone notices and gently guides him again to his original place in the line.

"Anyone for Hamburg at half past five?" a young man announces as he approaches us. He is tall, about six foot five, clean shaven, donning sunglasses inside the terminal, his uniform well pressed. A tie sits neatly around his neck and next to it hangs the coiled cable of his earphone. Hearing the word Hamburg from his mouth, you know he knows something important, though you don't know what it is. And just as quickly as he appeared, he went on his way. Maybe to search along the next lane.

Another text message: *Danny was looking for you. For the third time today. Where are you? And Martine, from the TV network? A producer. She has a new investigative reporting show. She left a number. Said you could call her back on Monday.*

I open the settings and change them so that the notifications stop jumping to the front of the screen and buzzing.

"Nothing like connections to save you a hundred bucks on a flight," says a young man. Bits of potato chips are crushed in the oval stadium of his mouth, sounding like the roar of a cheering crowd. He's part of a young couple with a stroller. His chest displays a Star of David. Still munching, he solemnly announces that there's no way he's taking it off in Madrid, not even when attending the soccer match.

"Dada, neck-shun neck-shun," his toddler coos, imitating his dad with admiration, trying to learn a new concept that is sure to serve him in the future.

About twenty minutes later, a lively conversation develops around the subject of cheap flights. As I reach the next row in the line, I notice a group of teenagers, all in white t-shirts and dark pants. They look like high school students. Here and there they shoot a selfie together. They're having a loud discussion with the *mochilera* about flight connections, laughing about experiences they shared on trips abroad with their parents.

"Anyone here for Moscow at six?" asks a curly-haired woman as all the stars align and I move ahead into the next spot in the line. She says nothing beyond that. She's wearing a red cord with a badge, the kind that gives her permission to detach the blue retractable belt from the stanchion post. The belt that designates the boundaries of the line. The badge that allows her to remain silent. A badge we will probably never get because we will never have the required security clearance. Whoever answers her is quietly asked to follow her.

And ta-da, as I argued at the beginning, the line is a living organism. There's a connection, a shared identity between its people. Even a tradition. Soon the President of the United States of America during World War I, Woodrow Wilson, will appear out of nowhere and demand the right of self-determination for this group.

"Excuse me, I'm sorry." Someone very gently puts a hand on my shoulder and asks me in English if I know what's going on with the flight to Hamburg.

"They came by earlier and asked," I say, trying to draw the agents' attention, but they're far away from me and can't hear.

"Aren't we flying via Hamburg too in the end?" asks the Star-of-David man, his hand feeling the depths of the bag of chips.

"We are," replies his wife.

"Well? This man says they've called it out. We're about to miss our flight." His thick voice becomes stronger.

"What are you yelling at me for? It's all because of your chips. You're so busy eating. And what about the child?

Won't you let him have any? Hurry up and find the guy who called for us before," she counterattacks.

"I'm hungry, I haven't eaten all day. And there aren't any left," he says, fingering the bag.

"Hello? Move ahead," the man says to the quiet man whose gaze is deep in the floor.

Together with someone else I try to assist a lady who is too polite to ask the staff. And, voilà, we all become a group on a common mission. Just like in a group dynamics exercise at a company's team-building conference.

"Anyone here with a connection to Montevideo?" A very short but very loud man suddenly emerges. He rolls the word 'Montevideo' the way you roll candy in your mouth, with all the accompanying accents.

"Do you know what's going on with Hamburg? It's half-past five. The la-dy here," Star-of-David man says, stressing each syllable, "and we are going to miss the flight."

The short man doesn't know, but still shouts to a group of agents at a distance from him. His shirt has some company logo on it. Not of an airline, maybe one of those that provides ground-handling services. He calls out 'Montevideo' once more until he notices a party of five waving and making their way towards him.

At this point, when I am no longer far from the security check, I find it difficult to take my eyes off the quiet man. The way he almost drags his feet. The way his handbag looks small but is heavy and bulging. I sharpen my gaze trying to figure out if I discern beads of sweat covering his face.

An unmistakable pair of long orange overalls approaches the line. "The Daring Explorers group ready to watch the Northern Lights—raise your hand," he cries, holding up a small square sign with a little twinkling star on it. A few individuals, men and women leave the line and go off with him.

Star-of-David, his wife and the young woman who doesn't speak English have an animated conversation with their agent, who assures them the flight won't leave without them. Star-of-David speaks out loud and strong.

The exchange of the *mochilera* and the high school students is momentarily interrupted by someone who looks like their teacher or someone in charge.

"As soon as we're done with security, dear children, you're free until ten to eight. And then I want you all at the departure gate, okay?"

It's finally my turn to check in. With my bag in tow, I rush to the security gate with the x-ray machines and join a whole new line. The quiet man, who is ahead of me, almost trips over his shoelaces. I am not imagining it. He really is sweating. I see little droplets and realize at that moment that the shiny blue layer covering him is a thin windbreaker. Even though it's winter, I am wearing a short-sleeved shirt and so is most of the line. It's seventy degrees Fahrenheit this evening, even indoors.

My mind goes from curiosity and even empathy to suspicion and, from there, to skepticism. Detached? Maybe stressed out? A jacket that doesn't make sense at this temperature? A heavy, bloated bag? My heart starts to beat faster. What's the script now, I think to myself. In thrillers, the hero thinks in microseconds. Should I say something to the security guard? Or maybe there's no time for even that? Can I even take the risk of shouting: "Beware, terrorist!?"

Our country is plagued by acts of terror. Mass shootings, stabbings, security incidents. Talk about crime running rampant in the streets. About the lack of governance. All this makes us jittery. The problem with screaming a warning is that, if it turns out the man is not a terrorist, it will be highly embarrassing. To me, of course. And in general. After all, we all sometimes think of terror scenarios. At that exact moment, after the explosion or close to it—a TV channel or radio station might come by or someone might take a picture for Instagram.

In a country prone to such violence, you must always have some make-up with you, something to fix your hair, a mirror. Some will also say a PR agent on call who can improve the text of your comments. To make it sound coherent enough to convey a message.

But no exclamation comes out of my mouth. I freeze. Meanwhile the quiet man is another step closer to his turn. One of his legs rises and moves forward while the other gets a little tangled in the shoelaces that curl up like the fringes of a shawl. He stumbles for a moment and my heart skips a beat, but catches himself and continues ahead with his heavy leather bag.

The line has now become very noisy. I decide that the security agent is experienced enough to recognize whether or not he's a terrorist. She takes the man's passport. She looks down, and then back up at him. Does her indifferent look mean she hasn't noticed anything suspicious? Or maybe it's reverse psychology? After all, if she suspects anything—she must act like nothing's going on. And now, as per the usual procedure, she asks him questions. I hear part of the conversation. The movements of the lips and my deep familiarity with this routine make me realize that the man was asked if anyone had given him anything to carry or check in for them.

The silent man looks back down. He reaches for the zipper of his windbreaker. I cringe. Why can't my mouth scream out? I'm sure his hand is shaking. He grabs and pulls the tab in slow motion. I'm already inhaling and getting ready to scream, but still nothing comes out. Now part of the jacket is open down to the chest. But he's not pulling out any bombs. He utters a few words. Maybe he's one of those ideological terrorists who have a statement to make: 'Ladies and gentlemen of the security personnel, how do you feel about having an attack today? With or without a monologue? Because I have these great Shakespearian metaphors and some socialist mantra about equal rights.' The agent frowns and looks at him. I think I hear the sentence: "What did you say? Can you repeat that? Did anyone give anything to carry or check in for them?"

He looks up, takes a deep breath, his hands rise and at once fall while his face contorts, and out of his mouth comes the voice of an Argentinian soccer commentator after a goal in the World Cup final: "Y-Y-E-E-S-S." The echo of his cry in the departure hall is thrown like a huge blanket covering the noise, the organized chaos, the sign carriers and the announcers of the calls to flights. Suddenly everything stops. Everything freezes. I cringe all over. Inspectors, security personnel, ground personnel behind the counters. Everyone is turning their heads trying to understand what all this is and what the fuss is all about. In an instinctive movement, the security agent raises neither a gun nor a TASER, but her hands to cover her ears.

Several of those standing in line try to storm in and

seize the man, but the tall security guard with sunglasses takes the spot by the female agent.

"Yes, someone gave me something to take with me," he says loudly. But without any confidence. Not as a statement, but in a broken voice. He sits down on the floor and unlatches the bag. The screams are now replaced by tears running down his cheeks, wetting his glasses. "She gave me something to carry for her," he repeats, pulling out of his bag some brochures and a thick book with a colorful hard cover. The security guard, still with one hand on the gun, tries to lift him gently to a standing position. "Why did she leave me? Why did she die? Why did she leave me to carry all this?"

The personal assistant suddenly emerges from the line.

"Can I help? He's with us," she says, "an employee of our company. We sent him on a surprise vacation. We wanted to help him clear his head a little. His daughter died unexpectedly. I will help with all the documents if needed. Come, Dillan, I'm here for you."

The agents are trying to deal with the situation and also to restore order. Little by little the hall returns to sizzling at the right volume.

"All is well. Please move forward," announces a shift manager in charge, who appears out of nowhere.

Now it's my turn. I approach another agent, submit my passport, and the questions begin:

"Did you pack on your own? Did someone ask you to carry anything for them? Or give you anything to pass on?"

I want to reply that I hadn't really packed my bag myself. That while I was packing, so many irrelevant items packed themselves into my carry-on bag—a small blue trolley with lots of zippers and hidden compartments. Entire scenes played out under fluorescent lights in the offices of one minister or another, advisor or activist. Director or advertiser. Strategist or journalist. Dialogs that were Gordon Ramsay-style gourmet delicacies when they just came out (there's nothing like the aroma of a campaign fresh out of the oven) but, over time, became leftovers of words and sentences that were buried like a sandwich forgotten in the bottom of a school bag.

"I'm asking because somebody may have tried to pass on to you objects that are forbidden by law, or that may harm the security of the flight and endanger others, with you being unaware. And it's okay if you didn't know that," she repeats the mantra.

I want to say that I really wanted to pack by myself, but couldn't. On the contrary, so many somebodies had passed things through me. And sometimes I wanted to keep them.

And now I can't do it anymore. I want to hand over several old bombs. A few rusty landmines.

We, the angels of destruction, worked on them. Just in case. Sometimes we handed them over to the guards, sometimes we detonated a controlled explosion. Or just the opposite. All of a sudden, when it worked in our client's favor, let's say three weeks before an election, the public body parts of our rivals would be scattered in a wide dispersion radius, to use bomb-disposal squad terms. And sometimes they would add very graphic plastic descriptions of the particles of their consciousness splattered on the walls and remark that the ambulance would arrive too late at the scene, in order to make sure there was no chance of them coming back to life.

I want to throw some of them into the sea. Between the waves. And others I want to return without.

Let the locals enjoy them.

And there are things that I so wanted to have packed together... together with him. Just one more moment with him, of him looking at me with the lakes of those blue eyes which hadn't had enough time to fully sense the flawed maturity of this world.

The immigration officer glances at my passport and then looks up at me. I want to explain to her that the picture was taken five years ago. So much has changed in these five years. I don't look like that anymore. Have I changed or am I purer now? More genuine? Maybe I've grown up? Maybe I'm much more me or maybe it's the other way around. Maybe I'm hitching a ride on everything that happened and making life easier for myself, or maybe I'm under the influence of New Age books and Buddhist sayings.

Death changes you, or purifies you, or the devil-knows-what. It seems to me that death already changed me the moment I learned that Lake was sick. Parents are said to feel that their child was killed even before the hospital or the police manage to locate them and inform them of the tragic news.

That's how I remember that moment, that phone call informing me he was in the hospital. How I felt that jab, the little person living in my belly tying strings to the sides of my body and yanking them in tightly. All of a sudden, my radiant face, the one expressing satisfaction with the outcome of a meeting I attended just an hour earlier, oozed into my shirt and a strong fire lit up inside me about to burst out. How I fought to keep my gaze on the road ahead, but dark, glistening spots threatened to take over my vision. How I swerved to the side of the road and stopped for a moment despite countless vehicles honking nervously behind me.

It seems to me that the agent suspects I'm a phony. She says she'll be right back and consults with another agent. I gaze aside and see that the quiet man has already been removed. In his place I am surprised to discover that Big Guy and Curly Hair from the train are being eagerly interviewed by the agent on the fast track. How did I not see them before?

My security agent is returning. While she's signing off my passport, another agent asks Big Guy and Curly Hair: "Did you pack on your own? Did anyone give you anything to carry or pack for them?"

They hesitate. "There's something we need to tell you," he says unexpectedly.

"What are you doing?" She turns to him, surprised.

"We're not really going to the concert." Big Guy looks up for a moment. His long, light, messy hair cascades down, hiding one of his shoulders.

"What do you mean? Where? What concert are you talking about?" the agent asks impatiently.

"We're traveling abroad," says Big Guy.

"Do you see the line here, man?" The agent raises his left hand and spreads his fingers. "All this is waiting for me, and it's only for the flights in the next two hours. So tell me now what you were going to say. Because the fact that you are going abroad is kind of obvious to me." In the last sentence he looks like he just swallowed a lemon and his mouth is crinkling.

"We're actually smugglers," says Curly Hair, looking down at the floor.

"Smuggling is the other way around, baby," Big Guy corrects her. "We are actually flying abroad to take something that we're then secretly bringing back here. Without them knowing. Get it? But I'm not a criminal. I don't want to have a record." It feels like he's breaking down. From where I am, I even detect a little moisture in his eyes. He gently places a hand on his girlfriend's shoulder and tells her not to worry, that it's all going to work itself out.

"Listen, kids. I'm supposed to be polite, right? Are you testing my limits or what? Tell me what the story is and immediately after that I will call my shift manager and let him decide, because you're also minors. Over sixteen, yes, but not yet eighteen, right?" As he speaks, he lowers his voice and forces his shoulders down. Evidently he is trying hard to use the softest tone in his arsenal.

"We became eighteen a month ago. It's the Purple album," she blurts out.

"Not Purple. It's the Blue Album, dumbass." Big Guy loses it completely.

"What the fuck are you talking about?" Language is the last thing the agent cares about at the moment.

"Records. The Prometheus Band's records. The Purple Album, bro. One of these can cost like three hundred dollars apiece or maybe more. This is rare. We thought we would smuggle them into the country, but now we're beginning to regret it. Don't turn us in, bro."

Chapter 3

"The more varied our means of communication, the less we communicate."

Variation on a J.B. Priestly quote

The tension drops all at once, like air released from a balloon. The impatient agent rushes to restore order and get rid of the kids who are making the enormous workload at the airport even worse.

After the security inspection and the duty-free shops, I then realize the flight is delayed. I'm looking for a way to pass the time. I remember the book of short stories I bought a long time ago. I sit down in a cafe near my gate and order a cup of tea that costs like a whole box of Ceylon tea. At least give me a pitcher, please. The woman at the counter looks at me with indifference, but she indulges me.

At this point war breaks out. Fatigue starts to creep in. Even though I've already wrapped myself in a sweater, I'm cold. One moment I'm straining to concentrate on the short stories by the foreign author and, the next, my eyelids close and an image appears in my head—the two of us laughing at the gate just before boarding the plane for a family trip. Our last trip abroad before the onset of the illness. I wake up, read a one-page story, try to get to the end, but again my eyes become heavy and shut on their own. Now I am watching in my imagination the trip we went on for his sixteenth birthday.

Finally, the plane that will take us to Madrid is getting ready to take off at nine instead of six. I sit back and glance at my messages. Ten new messages. Four from the office, three from the assistant to the Minister of Social Affairs. Two consecutive messages from the digital consultant with reports on the new trends on social networks I asked him to send, in order to inspire the team. And another one, from the one and only—the client we always get back to, no matter what, wherever we may be, and at any time of day.

So I get back to him.

"Good evening," I say, as I walk on the jet bridge.

"A wonderful evening. How are you? Is everything well? Am I disturbing you?" He is always polite. A charmer. It's easy to be polite when the answer is obvious.

"Disturbing me? It's always nice to hear from you."

"I am sending you a document via email with the messaging we plan to release to the media ahead of the shareholders' meeting."

I don't interrupt him, but I try to interject right after the period at the end of the sentence, explaining that, "They surprised me, and I won't be available for a day or two due to a holiday abroad."

"Cool, no problem. Just deal with it soon, because, you know, there's that thing with the lady. Don't let it blow up in our faces." I wish him a good week ahead, and promise to get in touch as soon as I get back.

"And... listen," God always adds his dessert. "If everything goes smoothly and you turn this saga around as you promised you'd do, I'm sending you to the Caribbean. On vacation." His voice is deep and full of confidence. Not like an anchorman, more like a radio host you love listening to. Something with feeling. With emotion. "To the Caribbean, hear me? So start looking for a girlfriend to take with you on the trip. Get ready." He concludes and hangs up when the plane's engines are already growling on the runway.

We fasten our seat belts and take off. We stabilize at ten thousand feet and I start to wander the isles of the plane. The young woman who needs to go to Seville meets me as I relax my legs walking along the economy aisle and tries to strike up a conversation with me. She sometimes says the word father, and I hear a father that always splits into two parts, starting a little lower and ending a little higher, as Lake would say it. I'm no longer looking for suspects wearing windbreakers, and I'm unable to concentrate on anything for more than a few minutes. My grumpiness can't wait to get away, as far as possible from here, just like my impatience for this wish to come true.

It's almost 2:00 am and I'm in Madrid. I put myself in a taxi ordered in advance and twenty minutes later I enter the lounge of the hotel where I booked a room for the night.

"Good evening," the receptionist greets me.

"Good night, or maybe good morning. I have a reservation here through Booking.com."

"For one night? Your name?"

"Night? I would say I booked a visit here. I just came to visit this hotel, because in two hours I have to leave."

The joke has no effect on her. Maybe it's because of the lateness of the hour.

I get the keys, go up to the room. I make myself some more tea and get ready for bed. I'm cold again. It makes sense because it's currently 41°F in Madrid. I don't undress or shower. I just wrap myself in two blankets, set the alarm clock on the phone, and close my eyes. But I can't fall asleep. I make myself more and more tea, until I collapse, overwhelmed with exhaustion.

From the moment my eyes close, no more than a second or two elapse, or so it seems to me, until I hear the alarm. I interrupt Jethro Tull's flute in *Nothing is Easy* and hear a hesitant voice. "I missed my bus stop," he says. "I'm near City Hall, downtown. I didn't notice that I'd passed the station I should have gotten off at. And, apparently, my wallet fell out of my pants." I know he means his sweatpants because this funny kid always refuses to wear jeans. I get up in a panic. I want so badly to be a bit angry at him, at the little absent-minded professor, but then I drive late at night into the city center, and hug him. He will say that's unnecessary because he's not cold, even though he's wearing sandals in winter. And on the way back, he will tell me about his adventures of the day and laugh at my dad jokes. But then the clock goes off again. This time for real.

I glance at it—4:30 am. I wash my face, fix myself up but not too much. The taxi is waiting for me downstairs and takes me to the airport. To the departures area.

I'm headed for Tenerife. I picked this destination while I stood in the cemetery. Instead of the flat ground where tombstones are scattered around, I imagined there was a claw crane machine, the kind you come across at mall arcades, with a lever that drives the metal claws that grab plush toys in exchange for coins. It's several stories high.

Above is his tombstone. If I press the button, the giant crane will randomly lower its jaws and pull out a tombstone. I decide that the first letter in the tombstone is where I'm going.

I know. Nobody really gets the toy in these games. In my case, the odds are even lower. The crane picks the tombstone of Tabitha Nee Thornston, that is, the letter T.

So I play Categories. Places with the letter T. I rule out the expensive ones like Taiwan, or those that are too cold this time of the year like Tbilisi or Turin. The ones that are not that suitable for a spoiled man like me, used to modern urban surroundings, like Tonga. Also any that might be dictatorships and those that are unpleasant for security reasons or high criminality rates. Finally my eyes glide on the map towards a small island to the left of Africa, only a two-hour flight away from Madrid, and I zero in on the target.

Chapter 4

Caught in a stressful situation? Don't hide your feelings, express them. Be assertive and communicate constructively. If you don't externalize your emotions and feelings—don't expect others to recognize them without words. And finally, if you cannot avert a stressful event— try to change it. Maybe not really change it, but only change the way you choose to see it.

(The Stress Management Guide)

Another delay at the Madrid terminal. I look right and left, play with the combination numbers in the lock of my carry-on. I get up to walk around. Go to the bathroom. Return. The flight was supposed to leave at seven, but everyone is still here.

I turn my mobile phone over. Throw a half-eyed glance at the messages and emails. And, boy, are there emails. Quite a few of them. I struggle to turn it back over.

The phone rings again. God is on the line. This time I try not to answer. Ultimately, the ringing stops. He sends a text and asks me to get back to him because he just remembered something else.

A few minutes later. Another ring from my partner this

time. I get up from my seat and walk around a bit, but the ringing doesn't stop.

"Hello," I answer, convinced he can sense something is wrong.

"Return Ariana's call. She's waiting. She needs advice. A brilliant idea. The kind of show you know how to put on," he concludes and does not expect answers or dialogue. I promise to do so. I dial the client. I listen briefly to her request. She calls me 'Professor,' because that's what my partner calls me when introducing me to new clients. They admire my compulsive curiosity and my enthusiasm for new fields of thought, and that does the trick.

My partner called me professor from the start. In nature there are courtship seasons, and I've had my share too. Two of them. I'm a man with some life experience. Not a child. A responsible adult. Living in a good residential area. Going out on dates once in a while. I courted the authorities to formalize Lake's status after I took him in as an abandoned baby from a foster home.

It all began as a challenge, as a project. At the time the blues kept creeping up on me. Nothing touched me, nothing truly satisfied me or really made me happy. Not really. I read about how people enrich their lives and what research says about it. I practiced yoga. I was into reading. Music. Meeting people. All this added a lot to my life, but didn't really turn things around. Then I came across an article that explained that volunteering is key—a BMC study indicating that thousands of volunteers of all ages enjoyed significant improvement in their mental health. Improvements in both physical and mental parameters. Better blood circulation and a 'high' one can't attain using drugs. That's when I realized it was time for me to change jobs and that volunteering would be great for my mental health.

That's why I went out one evening with a friend who is active in the community. Over a beer and a glass of wine, we bingoed the names of causes I could join.

"Go as far as you can," I told her.

"The farthest?" she replied. "Aiding earthquake victims. Helping refugees who arrive by land or sea. Volunteering in a prison with murderers sentenced for life. Making them recognize the mistake they made by brutally taking another person's life. And maybe even working with the elderly—going to visit lonely seniors in remote areas and bringing them food. Help them get through the Welfare Agency's red tape."

We toyed with all these ideas for a bit until, late at night among boozy giggles, my friend came up with an idea: "How about joining an organization that takes care of abandoned babies who are only a few days old. Would you be in for that?"

"I could be," I say to her. "Wanna bet?"

"You're on. Because I have a friend who runs one."

The next day I'd forgotten all about the issue, but she hadn't. And so, in the end, I can't evade it. I note it on my calendar. I go see them. I do a SWOT for them. An analysis of strengths, weaknesses, opportunities and threats. But I feel like I haven't really volunteered. I just told them the same things I would tell any potential client. After a week I return to see the director of the organization and ask her what they need. Concrete stuff. Specific assignments.

I issue a standing order in my bank account for a monthly donation. A month later I become involved in the renovation project of the small shack that houses the organization. I raise funds for paint and furniture. I join the team that works on the garden, forge a driveway, help plaster the walls and feel excited with the final result. In the next stage, I regularly order diapers from a wholesaler with whom I've negotiated a large discount. A client of the office. Then the director of the organization suggests I come once every two weeks to take care of a baby. A real baby. A baby that just arrived.

Up to that day I had never touched children or related to them. As a child I was very shy. The fact that I was interested in history, philosophy, society and economics did nothing to make me 'cool' among my peers. In elementary school some of the kids ignored me. Others beat me up. I was the child who read about the Watergate scandal at the age of nine. And the fact that I hated soccer certainly didn't help.

An open transparent bassinet. Soft white generic sheets. I reach out my arms and lift 5 pounds against my chest. I cuddle a plushy chicken-yellow onesie, which meshes in well with the thin light downy hair. I am not afraid to bathe him. I place a supporting hand under the nape of his neck and place him inside the blue tub with the shallow water. It seems natural to me. Once every two weeks becomes once a week. Then every three days.

A few weeks later there's a follow-up evening with my community-devoted friend. I've won the bet. She treats me to dinner at a good restaurant downtown. We talk a lot, as we always do when we get together.

"I wanted to ask you something. As a mother of three with many motherly friends, I want to ask whether it's always like this or is it only in my case."

"What do you mean?"

"His eyes."

"Is anything wrong with them?"

"I don't know. Is it always like this?"

"How? You still haven't told me what the problem is."

"They aren't exactly eyes. I look at him and feel that they are gateways. Like sliding windows with a lake behind them." At the time I did not understand where those words came from.

"Do you realize you've mentioned him exactly every fifteen minutes in our conversation?" she replies. "I tempt you at the fanciest restaurant in town. I tell you about the $100 dollar Wagyu steak, the fine sorbet, and you keep going there. There is only one conclusion." She now directs a clear message at me. "He's the one who will fulfill you."

I try to laugh it off, to make a joke, but she is quick to push me back into the furrow. "This is it," she says confidently. "You need him to be with you."

We part at midnight. Despite the wine, I think about it for the rest of that night. I can't fall asleep. At 4:00 a.m. I recall something else. At the foster home, babies are assigned numbers for emergencies. But I don't call him 412. I call him Lake.

Over morning coffee after a shower and while buttoning my shirt, I come to the conclusion that I have nothing to lose. I was so unaware that I was convinced it was an experiment that could be reversed. Goods that can be taken home for a month's trial. You don't love it, you don't keep it. From that moment on, I did what I do best: crack a challenge. Courting governments and selling myself as a potential father though the adoption process. A process that was completed sometime later.

Seven years later, when Lake was already at school, the partner also began courting me. We would meet in cafes and try to be discreet because, after all, I was employed somewhere else. In the end, realizing that my career needed upgrading and refreshing, I acquiesced to his advances. I left my workplace and became his business partner.

"Until now you were playing with Lego, now you have reached the major leagues; plus, you are a great scoundrel," he said, meaning to flatter me.

On our third courtship date, my (then potential) partner placed a sheet of paper on the table with an offer for options and shares that would accumulate over several years.

"There are many good people in the market," he said to make his case. "You are highly professional, but I'm not taking you on because you were a VP of Client Services with my competitors. I follow the example of my uncle, whom I adore. He is the one who told me: buy a Mercedes Benz, a Rolex, a Hugo Boss suit. Drink only coffee made from Arabica beans, and then go pick the money off the floor. And he is also the one who said to me—have a professor next to you. One who is reliable. Knowledgeable. A wise intellectual. Loyal. Faithful."

And I am faithful. The fact that I don't have a PhD and have never taught at any academic institution is no obstacle, of course. I just need to look and sound like a PhD. And I'd better be wise.

"I brought the professor with me today and he has an amazing idea for you," was the first sentence my partner said when we entered God's dark office. God sat there with a cigarette between his lips and said nothing. My partner had warned me that it took him some time to warm up.

First you must go through the admissions committee. But if you prove your loyalty, you're in. And, once inside, it's great. God is our central axis. The captain of the national team. The one who introduced us to a dozen other clients. He is the one journalists incessantly chase. He is the one who can pick up the phone and call elected officials such as the Head of the Joint Economic Committee and go with them for a beer.

The crew announces the flight over the loudspeaker and we are asked to stand up. The stanchion belts are quickly deployed, creating five separate lanes. My hunger rises and so does my impatience. I pull out an apple and begin gnawing on it. The ground crew supervisor speaks in a loud, resonant voice that's drowned out by the poor acoustics of large airports. She explains that we will be divided according to row letters on the plane. "Research has shown," she says, "that this is the best way to guarantee you can board your flight faster and more efficiently." Yes. She repeats and stresses this. It's based on research.

My level of discomfort gets worse. I want so much to be far away. Anywhere that is furthest for me. At some point, the attendant gets closer to my lane, surveys the drill formation standing at attention presenting arms, with their trolleys. "Can you still hear me with your apple?" she asks/demands.

"I'm almost finished," I say and shove the rest of the apple into my pocket so as not to miss my turn.

From the large windows by the gate we watch the ceremony. As in any ceremony, the right of way is first of all for the silent. The chief porter appears with their load covered in a black cloth, tied to a procession cart. Four porters carry them ahead. The luggage no longer feels anything anyway. The porter has a whispered exchange with the attendant.

She lifts the veil for a moment and asks: "Sir, I'm just checking—is this yours?" The officiant makes a cynical joke about death, the kind that is only allowed to those who regularly deal with the dead. I imagine them casually throwing their luggage into the belly of the plane. May they rest in eternal peace.

While the porters advance forward, the signal is given and the convoy leaves. First people with disabilities, women with strollers. Each of them has been thoroughly scanned. My apple oozes juice that seeps in through the pocket lining, gluing it a little to the leg muscle and trickling down, tickling me slightly. After that, people in the seats corresponding to section C move forward and board the plane. Then B. And A. But then the chief flight attendant stops the ceremony and apologizes, saying that it was a mistake. She pulls out some of those who already walked through A and asks them to get back in the line again, because the ones who need to enter now are actually the people from section D and, only at the end, are the A's to board.

By the time it's my turn, after all these delays, when my vacation is so close and yet so far away, the attendant who mentioned the apple points to my carry-on bag saying: "Please put it in our baggage sizer. I'm afraid it's too big. We will have to send it with the checked luggage."

Just at that moment my cell phone buzzes angrily. This time it's a ring. Someone's calling. I draw it out of my pocket. It's the producer of a current affairs radio program. Seven is the exact time when they call nicely to talk about someone they want to interview this morning on an important topic. I press 'mute' and return it to my pocket. I'm thinking of about an hour or so later, eight or eight thirty, when the program goes on air. The interviewee will be waiting for the call but won't make it to the line-up because of news that comes in about a stabbing attack at the mall in Paramus, New Jersey. Speaking of the important topic? Several other people will receive the same phone call and hear the same speech this morning.

"How is that possible?" I ask too loudly, having reached the internal earthquake stage. "I've been traveling with this bag, an airplane carry-on bag, for ten years and it's never happened to me. Look," I say, trying a different angle with her and another staff member standing next to her. "Check the size of my bag. See the sizes allowed. This bag was designed to fit in a plane, in compliance with the standard."

"Sir, please don't argue with us. The fact that you have been traveling with this bag for ten years and, although you've been our customer for twenty, does not change what the law says." Maybe he was polite, maybe he spoke in a normal tone of voice—but I, the recipient of this message, only heard laws, powers of attorney, signatures.

"I'm not sending this bag," I assert firmly, feeling my heart beat faster. The condolences that rise up like bile, the mercury that expands in the narrow windpipe of standing-up-for-my-rights.

"Sir," this time the attendant is assertive and raises his voice a little. "If you continue to object, I have the right to keep you from boarding the flight on the grounds of crew safety."

"I'm not sending this bag." I pronounce the words

clearly, as I lean on the counter that separates the gate from the walkway that leads to the plane.

The attendant orders some people to move ahead. His superior addresses me. He managersplains that this is a final warning and it is time for me to relinquish and send the bag to the belly of the plane. "It won't cost you anything and you won't be delayed too long. You'll just wait at the baggage claim area. That's all."

I look right and left. The line is getting increasingly shorter, and I have no idea where this proposal comes from: "I want you to check all the bags. If you check all the bags, I'll send mine too," I say, running out of patience.

After a short consultation, they pull out a kind of metal cage. It has a rectangular base and side handles and is made up of a metal mesh with rounded corners, shiny and white. They ask whoever is left with me to place their hand luggage in the cage. One by one. We all become children trying to fit shapes through the holes, like in those games toddlers play. Quite a number of bags are not spared the harsh judgement and are ceremoniously sentenced to join mine in the belly of the plane.

Finally, the supervisor personally escorts me to the plane, to make sure there is no more trouble. "How do you see this incident, sir?" He asks me while we walk.

"I see it as an unnecessary game in a cage. A cage that keeps you shut in your inflexibility. You saw everyone's handbags, which were all more or less within the size. Not everyone with an extra zippered compartment is a criminal. You have shown inflexibility. You followed the rules, but you irritated and delayed all of us."

"A matter of perspective, I believe," he replies and directs me to my seat. "I believe that if you saw it the way we do, you would be less angry. May I ask why the gentleman is traveling to Tenerife?"

"Vacation." I reduce the answer to a minimum but then decide to expand it a little. "Actually, also to kind of disconnect a little from daily life, from work. You know. One needs to sometimes."

"Most of our passengers are leaving on vacation. I like to think of my work in this way: I help people reach freedom. I keep things within the boundaries here so that they can reach freedom safely."

I nod, trying to appease him. I fasten my seatbelt. Before the supervisor goes on his way, I call after him. "Excuse me, before you go—do you know what a Triangsquircle is?"

"A Triangsquircle?"

"It's an expression from a children's TV show about learning math. The Triangsquircle is a shape that consists of a triangle, a square and a circle. I saw the shape of the metal contraption, and wondered what name we would come up with for it. Do you have one?"

The agent straightens up, sighs and smiles. "We in the company call it 'downward facing dog.' If you look at the shape of the metal strips, you will see how fitting it is. It helps us relax."

Chapter 5

The engines heat up and the plane takes off. Madrid is left behind, giving way to the sea. Africa unfolds before our eyes, followed by the coastline of Morocco. I look out the window of the plane at the island that is getting closer.

Leaving the terminal, the smiles and the various services of an island that is used to tourists appear. The well-oiled machine of a car rental company. An attendant who quickly fills out forms and issues the lease documents. She gives out instructions in English, but it seems like they could be understood even without her uttering a single word. Lots of motioning and gesturing. On the car diagram, she points at where the spare tire is, the code needed to start the engine, the parking lot outside the terminal and a number with a letter—where the car is waiting for me. And one more voucher for a chain of gas stations that operates across the island where I can fill the car up at a discount. "Fuel's on you," she indicates. "You can return an almost empty tank." I smile back at her, take out my famous carry-on bag that had been languishing in the belly of the plane and step out into the air outside.

I am greeted by a huge sign. An orange-colored X with the bottom third of a circle symbolizing a smile. Like the marker on a map of an island with a hidden treasure. It says 100% Life, in Spanish. *100% Vida*.

I type the destination into the navigation system screen and start driving towards the first milestone on the way to my treasure island, which is my B&B, but regret it as I do so. I hope to find the treasure but I don't even have a map. Just an island from which you cannot escape to anywhere else.

I decide to introduce some rhythm, a mood, and build up a fighting spirit. I pick *House of Kings* by Focus in the car and shake my head to their dancing flute. Cruising down the only freeway while lightly touching the brake pedal to the beat, I turn east to a neighborhood that impresses me as being a quiet bourgeois area and swallow it with my eyes. I have to stop and make way for the tram to cross the main avenue.

Entering Santa Cruz de Tenerife, the capital, I feel a bit like Alonso Fernandez de Lugo, conqueror of the island. The regiments of seething discontent and protest within me are ready to storm the place. Like De Lugo in 1494 entering the city, they vanquished together. He and the Spaniards he led must have been purpose-driven and cold-hearted, otherwise how could they ignore the endless sea that extends before me as I drive down the road from the high mountain towards sea level?

I try not to let the spectacular view have any effect on me. Being a mission-oriented person with a daily routine, I turn to the task of gearing up. Already at the parking lot it's a different tune. The aisles in the supermarket make me drowsy. De Lugo? Por favor! That was hundreds of years ago. That's long gone. Now give us a break—they say, forcing me to be quiet. I move slowly between the sections: cheeses, vegetables, fruits, cleaning products, ready-made food. I end up in a line that isn't long. People are speaking Spanish. The bored cashier doesn't understand English.

I put the groceries in the car, slam the trunk behind me and get into my seat. I still have some time left until the B&B I booked becomes available. So what's the next task? What's on my schedule for the day?

I remember that a little over a week after the funeral, someone called.

"We haven't seen each other in a long time, I know, but I heard the news, and I had to get in touch to tell you how sorry I am for your loss." After a few questions he said that in such moments it is important to be on the move and do things. To work yourself to infinity and beyond. That's what helped many of his friends. Channel everything into positivity. Fine, but what does someone who already runs three times a week do? Someone who is busy running new initiatives and campaigns? How much busier can they get?

It reminds me of a well-worn joke:

"I don't feel well, Doctor."

"I can't find anything wrong with your health," the doctor replies. "Maybe you need to get fresh air more often. Move. Walk. Keep going, in rain or shine."

"But Doctor, I am a mailman."

I now notice a gas station nearby. Thank God, another assignment. I stop. Fill up the tank. A light sea breeze. The Sun. The saleswoman at the convenience store offers me a discount coupon for tourists so I can fill up gas at their chain. I walk around the store for a bit, looking for something interesting.

Back in the car. The fuel nozzle fills up the tank. I sit down in the passenger seat and wait. I scroll through old messages on my cell phone. I open the weekly newsletter of an expert in economics and capital markets, only to get stuck on one striking phrase: 'Going against the trend. Those who went against the trend made a profit,' it says there.

I return the nozzle to its hook, get into the driver's seat and lean back. I start the car and begin driving into the city, with that sentence stuck in my head. I have always been a missionary preacher when it comes to crisis management for my clients. I often found they were distracted and confused. The millionaire who is embarrassed by the risk of his name being mentioned in connection with a possible deal with a well-known sports venture. The business leech who is trying to figure out how to keep recurring malfunctions in her company's products from bringing about its collapse. The friend who discovers his business is in the middle of a hostile takeover. The politician who fails to cope with a typhoon of baseless accusations splattered at him.

Reduce the room for uncertainty, I would tell them. Let's sort out our thoughts for a moment. Let's review what we know and what we don't. Let's build an orderly strategy. Let's look for the levers. Let's map the arenas. Let's speak out with one voice.

Like an old, seasoned veteran fox, I tried to tame my private typhoon, abiding by the tried-and-true rules, and reducing the dimension of uncertainty. I filled my pockets with heavy stones from a headstone and a funeral procession. I put it in the line of those offering condolences. A cordoned line with retracting belts and designated groups.

My friends from college. From politics. From business deals. Friends from work. From the community. From the gym. For days on end. Each time I asked the typhoon if it could please leave me alone and allow me to pack in peace, but it didn't answer and went right on swirling in circles around me.

After days of mourning, with so many guests coming to pay their respects that I had to bring the chairs from the porch into the house to seat them, I put them back outside. But the typhoon wouldn't go back out. I couldn't even squeeze it into a closet. It remained an angry, busy, raging bull. Left with no other choice, I activated the Judgement Day armament. I planned tasks. I managed time. I set goals. I analyzed data. I didn't have time to feel sad. I built a greenhouse, but the typhoon blew it away. Time and time again it brought devastation upon the frail seedlings of my sorrow. I hastened to place scarecrows of events and birthdays, jokes and ordinary slips on banana peelings among the furrows of my heart.

Legions of rodents invaded my nights. Images flashed like lightning and struck me. It turns out lighting can strike in the same spot again and again. I woke up to sleepless days that followed sleepless nights. I walked among the crowds as an isolated bubble, my muscles feeling the memory of the effort of carrying his weight as he became more and more physically dependent on me. I have an old photo of us running together in a 10K charity run. Just a few years later he is sick and withered. Limping away with a stick. Another two months go by and he confidently leans his weight on his father. Because Dad will hold him and keep him from falling. He leaned again and again throughout the entire period the tumor embedded in his brain blocked and stopped motoric activity in his body, until everything was seared as an eternal seal. Until every part of my body cried out for sleep and I plunged into my bed.

A small moist drop collects at my tear triangle, rubs itself for a moment on the surface of my eyeball blurring my vision as I drive, my mind churning the memory that made me run off to this place. I'm being honked at from behind because the traffic light is now green.

And maybe it really is time to blur the vision. To drive on the green light, but against the flow. Maybe it's time to increase the room for uncertainty. To decide not to make any decisions. To go against all habits, against all schedules. To deny, mainly. Not to sort. To place a bucketful of options in front of me, and not necessarily choose any of them. To keep busy occasionally and to not keep busy at all. Maybe those who are busy, those who plan, those who spend all day managing their time and counting the minutes must stop planning in order to find the treasure?

To leave everything for a moment and let go, whatever may happen—to fall, to fall apart. To not answer when the flood calls. And even if it sends an email—there will be an on-vacation auto reply. Right now— the deluge is after me. We'll talk about everything later.

On particularly busy days I would leave the office and go to some show in the most remote pub I could find, or head to an art gallery and look for inspiration. Sometimes, if it gave me a good idea, I would buy a piece. In our storage room there are around twenty or thirty of these, covered in cloth.

Now I stop the car in one of the streets of the city. Park

in the Rambla and Santa Cruz park area and stroll around to look for inspiration.

One moment I'm a fish, like the imposing bronze Chicharro sculpture, a horse mackerel over three feet long rising from the edge of a high wave. A gift from Venezuela to Tenerife. I stand next to it, mimicking its mouth opening upwards, in a classic Instagramy duck-face sort of way.

Basically, like many of the residents here, I too was a kind of fisherman in my life. The thing with the fish in our profession—especially with politico clients—is that they really crave the limelight. But they don't think about the consequences. One of which, for example, is to end up on the plate of a wealthy diner in a fine restaurant.

The current Chicharro also had its share of adventures. In the year 2000 it was stolen, made its way to continental Spain, and was rescued just before it was smelted in Valencia.

Then I lie prostrate like Henry Moore's *El Guerrero de Goslar*, cast for a moment as a hero who fell in battle, his shield lying at the bottom of his feet. I hope it's not my treasure trove because, in that case, one should stop here. I didn't come all the way here to fall in my battle.

At noon I park in the circular area of the city square, which has a fountain in the center. I look in admiration at *El Guerrero*, a tall, black, naked figure. He is poised to guard me and the whole island, together with his partner, the ten-foot-plus giant standing next to an ancient city gate on the other side of the square. His hands are resting on the sword under his knuckles and his gaze is piercing ahead.

I go back to the car. The navigation system directs

me along the boardwalk to the large wave-shaped auditorium. From there to the beach. The golden beach of Teresitas. I stop for a moment, place my buttocks on the sand first and then lie down completely. My head leans back. I blink at the sun that's racing towards the approaching sunset.

You get it, ladies and gentlemen, look at the pictures in the presentation I've prepared for you. We at the office always bring with us a presentation. Look at this strip, the rare volcanic natural reserve with underwater animals and plants unique to the area. Are you watching the film about angel sharks? The video is a bit choppy because the internet here is weak.

Can you move to the next slide please? Here, the Spanish army divided the Teresitas coastal strip into three sections: The first strip belongs to the village of Andrés whose residents have gone to the beach to take a dip, eat ice cream, and sip drinks before the sunset. The next slide shows the second coastal strip, where a group of Moors, Moroccan people sent from the other side closest to Africa, chose to settle. And the third strip of beach is for the royals: the Princess of Orléans and Duke Karl who bathe separately from the commoners.

And now I come to the point I want to make. A beach is a matter of branding. Everyone in the profession knows this. The municipality of Santa Cruz schlepped 270,000 tons of desert sand from the Sahara on its back so it could be photographed to show the world how wonderful it is to vacation here. Those are the kind of ideas we bring to the table in our company. That's our added value. That's why you should hire us as your advisors.

I give myself a few more minutes to enjoy the afternoon sun and then get back up, shake the sand off my clothes and continue in the car to the narrow road to El Suculum that overlooks the beach above. It is a short climb of less than a mile; from there it is a sharp bend and particularly narrow streets. There's no denying it. The sunset does the trick. It is so spectacular that you have to try not to fix your gaze on the view lest you accidentally find yourself approaching the beach again, just not in the way you wanted.

I can barely squeeze through between the sidewalks. I stop the car to get out and look at the narrow street to figure out the optimal way to park and still let others pass through. On the brink of darkness, I turn off the engine and go out onto the densely packed hot asphalt, leaning against the walls of the tall houses. I hear the pitter-patter of Lake's feet and laugh. Galloping, as he sometimes would in long, narrow spaces, shouting "Corridor, corridor!" like a loudspeaker system announcing that someone was coming through. I involuntarily get down on my knees. His horse-runs always end in a hug, with me inhaling his sweat and smile.

Chapter 6

A Code

When exactly did this happen to me? What had been the exact Archimedean point? The place where flour and water became the glue that made me stick to this little guy?

After that meal when I finally decide to take him, my sails fill with a fighting spirit. But, within a few weeks, it all turns around. Like something you crave but, "once it's yours, it no longer interests you. During the first months I rarely talk about him at the office. I hide his existence. I get into a routine of diapers, a bottle, a bath and a nanny who comes in the morning and leaves in the afternoon. Then I have a meltdown. One morning I go see the director of the foster home and tell her it's not working out.

"What's wrong?" she asks, laughing.

"I'm sick of this. I got the idea. I don't think he's making me feel any better, so I'm returning him, okay?"

She's rolling on the floor laughing, clutching her stomach. "You're so adorable," she says, "you're the best."

"No, I'm serious. Dead serious. It's not working out. Take him back." She finds it hard to grasp the idea. It takes maybe fifteen minutes for her to realize that I really mean it.

Then she sits me down and talks to me like no one has ever talked to me before. A combination of a social worker and a police-interrogator in a case involving the welfare of a delinquent neighborhood boy who got involved in crime. She leaves me speechless, shocked, saying there is no way back. It is irreversible. You did the deed, didn't you? Now you're fully responsible.

Rarely in my new dad-adulthood do I manage to mumble only a few words. I leave the place shocked and pained, as they say in obituaries, about my premature departure. Angry at it for not explaining the meaning of the matter to me, but actually angry at myself for being such a clueless child. Time replaces resentment with a renewed routine. An assignment. Something I will have to bear. I feel like I messed up big time. Instead of it making me a better person, it stops me, and even sends me into further decline. It will also hurt my creativity and my work. I feel like I got out on the wrong side of life. I rack my brain with the question of how to get out of this situation, knowing perfectly well that there is no way out, unable to come to terms with my fate. What a fatal mistake.

Only looking back do I recognize how my new routine took a turn. When you're in automatic mode, visual illustrations tend to creep up. Lake can sit. Then stand. He shows the first signs of expression. He utters his first words. He makes faces. And no, back then I didn't get all excited the first time he said "Daddy."

Today I know that, subconsciously, I had been waiting for it. Today I know that I learned a new language. Today I know that that was the start of a communication code between father and son. A code that defined common phrases we used. A child asking his dad to bring him things from the grocery store, or small habits formed in the playground, with an outstretched hand, on a weekend outing. Things I had never done before.

In real time I continued to treat this as if it were a normal routine having no effect on my life. As if there was nothing special here. Just like when police officers say to a crowd: "Nothing to see here, folks, you can move on."

He goes to daycare and then preschool. He starts to talk about other children. I am not active in the PTA, nor a member of any committee. Occasionally we have to meet moms, because Lake wishes to play with a friend from kindergarten. And here and there a conversation takes place. Sometimes even a pleasant conversation. One day a mother approaches me to say that since Birch and Lake play so nicely together, we should arrange a playdate.

I relent and arrive at a garden apartment in the suburbs of the city. A battered car is parked in the garage. The place is messy. The children click instantly. I shudder at the disarray, but she is actually well-groomed and pleasant. Unwittingly I get dragged into a conversation with her and forget about the children's existence. She pushes a strand of hair behind her ear and looks at me with very large, dark eyes. She asks me questions in a very soft, feminine tone. Then she talks about her divorce. I express sympathy. We exchange witty jokes about the life of single parents raising young kids, with no social life, no going out, no meeting potential partners.

The second time Lake comes to Birch, they are swept up into his room right away and the conversation with his mother heats up in seconds. Within twenty minutes she touches me gently, and from there the way to the bedroom is short.

"Don't worry," she says as we kiss, "Birch's room is a safe space, there's no way anyone can get hurt in there or anything. And they can play on the computer for hours." But who cares? I stop thinking about Lake in an instant, because I am released from the shackles at last. He doesn't exist now. He was obliterated by the need to fuck her.

I ignore the clothes scattered on the bed, unbutton her dress and then I give up and undress her from the top. Her hands are under my t-shirt. She caresses my back, then takes off my belt, unbuttons my pants. She slides them down.

I kiss her face, her ear, her neck. My body is boiling. She is very gentle, but I am not. Not at all.

Her gaze the day after. As opaque as a wall. The termination of engagement. Birch pulled away from Lake. No more playdates, even though the two went to elementary and high school together. I still saw her at parent-teacher meetings and year-end celebrations, but not beyond that.

That gaze only resurfaced after Lake's funeral. Only then did I realize I did not receive it with indifference. Only then did I realize that I had it well cataloged in the list of things I would like to give someone else to pass through for me, like the security agents asked about at the airport. Just so that I don't have to carry all that weight alone.

"I was convinced we were starting something," she whispered to me in the hallway leading to the bathroom while some of my colleagues sat in the living room laughing at an inside joke. There was no escaping her.

"You were so charming the whole time," she went on, saying things one does not say to a person in mourning. "And suddenly you no longer heard me." A small tear fell from her eye, smearing her makeup. "I told you I liked it, but slow. To take it slowly, gently. And suddenly, without any warning, you became a wild animal. You ripped my panties. You laid me on the bed and we fucked like two animals that just wanted release." Oh my God, how can anyone say those words in such a place, even in a whisper? A few feet away from her stood a ninety-two-year-old friend of my mother's who had insisted on coming. I was trapped.

This was my reality. The instrumental reliever of needs, the goal-oriented business developer without unnecessary emotions who works the whole way. Here and there a routine service maintenance with some divorcee, but no more than that.

And yet, somehow more and more strings are attached to this boy. Deceit is essential in warfare. Maybe because these were tricks I didn't know. It seems the final die was cast in the white room with the white bed. The window, without any blinds or curtains, shone with light. A white table. A cool, bright plastic chair. An hour in the waiting room and then five minutes inside. Lake was three and a half years old.

"Well, we've run all the tests and he needs double hernia surgery. It's not a big deal. You can make an appointment for this summer at City Hospital," said the doctor. A clinical, surgical statement. For him, the code was clear. His basic premise was that this was matter-of-fact and that there was no real point in non-verbal communication. So, while briefly saying what he said, he made sure to continue typing up the consultation documentation into the computer.

However, my pheromones reacted involuntarily to the medical antiseptic that heavily permeated the air. A heaviness that includes disdain—disinfected disdain. My receptors sensed a small hit on the wing. At least that's how I felt then. Just a light hit.

Thus, for the avoidance of doubt, I stuck to the principle of respect and transmitted all the signals indicating that the doctor and I were fully calibrated and synced and that there was no problem whatsoever.

I added an understanding look plus a joke and a smile, since we lacked an exclusive common code that was as impossible to fake as a peacock spreading its tail to secure the attention of the females.

He gave me a sheet of paper with an arid surgery order document without aftertastes or flavors at all, all this aiming to achieve some savings for the HMO. Lean and generic. The text was just right, with just the compulsory words. In my mind I continued to believe that it was a slight hit in the wing. I trusted the procedure but, deep down inside, I felt I had been handed sandpaper that made my hair stand on end like porcupine quills.

There is no doubt that the doctor succeeded in his goal to not give any message to Lake who was sitting with me. And so the recipient of the non-message interpreted it as an opportunity to spend a pleasant hour with dad. He followed the pattern of the cobblestones, counting the steps as he skipped down them with joy.

It was March and, after a rainy night, the day was pleasant. We went out to bask in the disorderly heat of the street. We walked together, I in the Bigfoot key, the man in charge. He, in the Littlefoot key. I pilot the cosmic aircraft of the Family System in my head. All the vessels in the fleet. Across all the considerations needed to be weighed. A bird's-eye view. And Lake absorbs the whole world below. He is poised on the runway. Just waiting to learn about all the flight instruments of life in order to grasp the steering systems later on.

On 3 Pine Street, my plane crashed and I tripped over a bunion lying on the sidewalk. I made an emergency parachute landing. Lake asked if I was okay. I said I was. I gave him a hug. I got up.

On 5 Pine Street, my pheromones celebrated the fruity scents of citrus trees, which were battling the smells of gasoline.

"Dad, can we get some orange juice?"

"Sure."

"What size would you like?" asked the vendor. I ordered a large glass and a small one. Lake asked how I knew how much juice was in each cup. We held an academic discussion on sizes and how to measure the contents of each glass using visual aids and feeling the oranges in front of us. We wondered how many spherical oranges it would take to produce juice for the cylindrical glass. We tried to guesstimate. The seller looked impatient. He was more interested in the end result than in our debate. After an information-based decision making process, we decided to go for two large glasses. Lake followed with great interest the vendor who expertly cut the oranges, and the machine that made sawing sounds.

I turned to look at the street. The sun's radiation, which lasered onto a mirrored glass window that reflected the mood of the street in elongated distortion, and returning a blazing glare that struck a bull's eye, passed through the screen of my sunglasses and settled on the retina and cornea in a burst of black bubbles. Upsetting the balance. Shuttling between the brain and the nose, between the nose and the mouth. Between consciousness and awareness. Between thought and emotion.

For a moment I thought I had just had a heart attack. Maybe an epileptic fit or had been struck by lightning. It happened in the blink of an eye. Until a tear rolled down from my eyes. One hand gripped the front of the counter. I didn't know if Lake noticed the storm. I sat down on the lone small wooden chair next to the kiosk, perhaps intended only for select regular customers.

Lake looked at the scented pile of fruits on display.

"Can we order a carrot too?" he asked.

We asked for a carrot. The vendor complained that he was done and how much time could be spent on juice sold for two dollars.

I seated Lake on my lap. We savored the orange-carrot mix. I tightened the grip of my hand supporting the small body that was sucking the juice. Closing his eyes, licking his lips and sucking from the straw with his puffy cheeks. As if ignoring the rest of the world. Disconnected.

Chapter 7

The apartment I booked in advance is modest and pleasant. It is wedged high up like an ancient Lego cube into a narrow, upright structure. Bricks and red tiles. Lego blocks placed about a yard apart from one another. In other words—your neighbor hanging their clothes to dry right next to you forms part of the view. And if you have to ask: Excuse me, can I borrow a cup of sugar? The distance is absolutely reasonable for passing it over to you above the street. It can almost be handed to you. Fresh eggs? Better not try.

The only problem is that, from the first moment, something here makes me dizzy. Even nauseous. I walk around the apartment, looking for the source. I open the wooden cabinets.

Meanwhile I think of tea. I push the ON button of the range, put on a small pot of water, and continue in my search for the cause of the smell. Five minutes later, I go back to the range, but nothing has happened. I haven't turned it on. I try again, but can't activate the burner. I press this button and that, I turn the knobs both ways. My movements become faster and more jittery, more confused. I bang on the vent hood, pull the plug out of the socket and put it back in, faster and faster like the train to the airport, going from a slow movement to 70 mph of searching, until finally I slam my wrist furiously on the hood and wait for a muffled noise to express my desperation. I call Joel, my landlord, to come. He speaks almost no English, but he is far from being as emotional as I am. His explanation is a mix of vigorous hand gestures, Spanish and a few words in broken English. He patiently conveys to me that the burners have a childproof safety device, and then easily releases what I struggled with for such a long time.

I open my carry-on bag and then try to open the closet doors, only to fail once again. My fingers slide over a button that opens the lock, and again I am in trouble. I call Joel again, who calmly explains to me how to deactivate the child lock. Again using a variety of gestures and a few words.

I finally sit down to drink the hot tea. I sip while trying to connect to the Internet for a moment, so I can check messages. This time I have trouble with the password, and discover that I'm really, really cold. The extra sweater on my body isn't helping either.

I call Joel for the third time. He manages to remain kind, shows me the password—it's written on the fridge. Right in front of me. How did I miss it?

He looks at me but I don't understand what he is trying to say.

"Un momento," he says and returns with another warm blanket. With movements of his hands he tries to tell me something, but I don't get it.

After he leaves I have an idea. I lean under the sink and discover the strong smell of something reminiscent of cockroach spray rising from underneath. It isn't an ordinary smell. What's more disturbing is that all the cutlery is there too. I'm debating whether and how to tell him about the smell, after having called him so many times.

Joel walks through the door. He does not lose his smile. The little hair he has, scattered on the sides of the head Einstein-style, moves back and forth as he tries to tell me something even before I have stated my need. "Ah," he exclaims suddenly. "I know to say. You have fever."

"Fever?" I'm afraid this might be a Spanish to English translation problem again.

"You sick," he repeats. I feel myself and wonder how I hadn't realized it before. I'm on fire, absolutely burning with fever. My nose is runny and stuffy. All along the way I have been asking everyone to repeat their words because I couldn't hear. I'm simply sick.

"Go rest," he instructs me and leaves me the keys.

My evening plans to go out to the town collapse. In real time, I felt dizzy. In retrospect, I know I didn't really unpack the suitcase. I didn't put the groceries in the fridge. I didn't shower or take off my clothes. I lay down on the bed and fell asleep.

Chapter 8

On a Mission

A student housing unit, 25 years ago. I hadn't slept. Again. I often feel like the light bulb in a fridge. When the door is closed, there is no light inside but, as soon as you open it—whoop, the light goes on, pale but enough to tell the cheese spread from the pot of stew or the vegetables. It emits light but not heat. And perhaps even when the refrigerator is closed, the light inside is on, but no one can tell for sure.

There are times like this, I try to reassure myself. But what times are we in now? Everything is fine. All is well. I go out in the evening with college friends. I hang out. I meet a woman here and there. I date her for a bit. Not for too long. So what times are these now? What period? What am I forcing myself to look for? And, in general, I'm not a person of the cold. I am a man of heat. So what is it, this dreaminess again? Once again, the feeling of disconnection from life, as if I were in a parallel universe.

My first memory is of heat. I was four or five years old, in long white pajamas with small animal prints. Usually giraffes. Dawn, uniquely quiet. My home is on the third floor, no elevator. Just blue-gray exterior stairs. The sun peeks through the blinds, casting beams of light on the outer wall of the parents' bedroom. I'm sitting on the living room floor, leaning quietly back against the wooden wall like an iguana in the Galapagos sun.

"He could sit alone for hours and play all by himself," the aunts used to say about me before pinching the tender cheek hard, right next to my blue eyes whose depth, innocence and, to a certain extent, tinge of sadness, captivated anyone who looked at them. I refused to comb my straight black hair. Every time Mom fixed it, I would tousle it back. Or I would feel ill all of a sudden whenever it was time to go to the barber shop.

Fourth grade. I don't open my mouth. The teachers are impressed by my large, clear handwriting. A rounded, innocent handwriting. But they don't know that I multitask: I write the minimum required and do a lot of daydreaming. During recess, I walk off calmly with small steps and leave the school's premises. I know how to plan it exactly. There's enough time for me to walk to the lake. I sit there on the same rock, which takes another minute. That leaves me ten minutes, sometimes eleven, to observe the activity in the water. A fictional series starring tadpoles, minnows, insects, and beetles. I squint hard until my eyes become fixed far beyond the jumpy plot. Until the modern Seiko watch Dad bought me for my birthday starts beeping. Sometimes it beeps for a whole minute before I snap out of my reverie and dash back to school. I manage to get through the gate at the last minute, after making sure to leave an apple or whatever's left of a snack there for the guard who fires words of exhortation at the weird boy who went to pay his private puddle a visit.

Junior and senior years. The first shaves in the shower, acne scars and the gaze of blue eyes in front of the mirror. I go to parties and sometimes to clubs, but dance very little. Tons of daydreaming again. This time it's a different technique. Absorbed by the music and the lyrics, which I mostly knew by heart and sang to myself. Staring at the walls. I would stay there until the lights went out, and go home in the wee hours of the morning, quietly humming The Cure's *Friday I'm in Love*, but don't really see anyone's shoes or watch them eat, or Bryan Adams's *Before the Night is Over*. Sometimes I would stop at a 7ELEVEN, and outside, a young man would be standing there together with two or three prostitutes who made some bitter statements about life with jokes I didn't get. As I listened, I'd buy some greasy hot dog or fried chicken, and gnaw on it until 4:00 am.

One time a girl, just one, asks me to dance with her. She explains it saying that I must be the only guy here who showers regularly and cares about smelling good. I look at her with my blue eyes and swirl into hers in my own inner vortex, almost hypnotized. The pupils turn in their orbit until we're no longer dancing in the club. We're wading in a puddle. My steps are engulfed in a song that has been my favorite ever since. I hold her. She smiles and breaks away from the dance, forcing me back to reality. Wanna go make out at the beach?

We dive into my parents' car and drive away. My gaze zigzags between the route to follow on the road and the trajectory that begins in her eyes, continues down to her neck, and reaches her cleavage. Once again, I'm dreaming. Once again, my pupils turn inside the sockets of my eyes—and boom. I climb onto the curb, almost losing control of the vehicle. The traffic police officers help me change the flat tire on both front wheels. I am asked what happened, if everything is okay. "I'm sorry. I was just staring at the frog in the puddle," I try to explain. The officers look at each other. The girl quickly slips away and takes a taxi home. My night ends at the beach, playing music on a tape to myself. I watch a group of boys trying to rescue an old Ford that has reluctantly turned into an all-terrain vehicle in the sand.

I decide to enlist in the military. On the first day of basic combat training, I am as confused as everyone else. Dragging myself and a bag with my belongings at night. Dazed from the lack of sleep and lack of understanding. Tormented left and right. Ultimately, I end up in some dark corner that smells of gasoline for cleaning guns and oil cans, and get a grumpy order to take oil from the containers and fill what is needed in the APCs and Jeeps parked there, each according to its type. And for f-ck's sake, put the right oil in the right vehicle.

In the background, the noise of the crickets plays a melody for me and with its help I memorize the numbers written on the gray front of the cans, indicating which type of oil is suitable for which vehicle type. Two gallons: 7064, 2032, 5044. The army marches on the iron stomachs of these crude war monsters capable of crushing rocks, but which require a sudoku of oil-type numbers, lest their sensibilities be filled with OSHKOSH oil instead of M113.

For some reason, new conscripts must sign for all the items they receive during night hours. For some reason, the sergeant likes me a little too much for my liking. And, for some reason, time stands still. At midnight I sign for the mess tin, and then get sent by the corporal to sign for an extra canteen. Then I run to the armory because I find out I've lost an empty cartridge. I don't understand the concept of *Brothers in Arms*. I don't understand what a *Melting Pot* or *Armageddon* is. I don't understand mottos. I'm exhausted enough to want to sleep.

Straight to bed, no shower. My next-bed neighbor says that two minutes in the shower are equivalent to two hours of sleep, yet I prefer to perch deep down under the prickly blanket. I close my eyes and, fifteen minutes later, I open them a slit to the sound of the neighbor's shoes dropping as he gets into bed.

In the end I fall asleep and have no problem getting up in the morning. Out of anxiety, fear, a basic lack of understanding of the social situation, all one big spectacle. The platoon commander, who appears only rarely, emerges after everyone is standing erect. The same commander who demonstrates how to charge at the enemy using a 40-pound weapon. The sergeant looks at him with admiration and blurts out a banal "What a warhorse!" referring to the size of the commander thundering the determined thunder of the battle; to the hair of his shaved head; to his animal-like masculinity—six-foot-seven with broad shoulders; wearing combat boots; about his navy-seal past; and to his name, unlike any other Tony Rambony. So what is he doing in such a low-league bootcamp? There are stories about an injury in a daring operation that left him partially deaf.

"Run, pretend it's your neighbor's lawn," he shouts at me. I, who can barely see in the dark, try to muster all my imagination to get through this nightmare. "Everyone here ran like a gazelle, and only you ran like an anteater."

I wonder where that came from. Whence emerged such a burst of metaphoric creativity at three o'clock in the morning, in the rugged hills near an unnamed town.

Half an hour later everyone is in their tents. Our orders are to sleep. I'm in the sleeping bag, but I can't fall asleep because of the tense anticipation. Waiting for an unspecified group of soldiers to soon enter the shaky tent propped up by stones, thorns and toothpaste. Ultimately, as a bonus, they'll piss on my leg. Contrary to the famous saying—I won't say it's raining.

When things get tough, I open my favorite essay book again and read. In the dark, with sore eyes. Martin Luther King's essay on refusing to obey orders. And in the morning? I don't feel well and I have a stabbing pain in my back.

"Go on the march!" the sergeant blares at me.

"I'm not going," I say.

"You're not?"

"I can't. My throat is burning."

"So are you refusing an order?" he continues to thunder.

"I am not refusing to, I just can't," I say and that's it.

Tony Rambony sentences me to twenty days on probation, and I walk around with a string and a small iron rod instead of a weapon. But I don't get any applause. I am not Martin Luther King, nor Gandhi, nor any of those famous conscientious objectors. Neither is my bed neighbor, Michael Jackson, who's neither the singer, nor his relative, and does not even dance, who went on a rampage with a knife because one of his mates became angry at him for not having the weapon ready in time for it to be cleaned. The next day, Michael disappeared from view and returned to the barracks two days later as a decorated hero, smiling from ear to ear. "They lost me for two whole days and couldn't find me." he whispered in the tent. "I really showed them." Michael received admiring glances from everyone, including the nerdiest ones, who patted him on the shoulder softly so as not to irritate him.

I didn't earn any insults either. In fact, I didn't earn anything, and that's that. I walked around with the rusty iron for another day or two. I haven't gone to the bathroom all week. Only at home, at my parents' place, completely exhausted, I place the fragments of my body on the toilet seat for a while after 'a shower worth two hours of sleep,' and then collapse on the bed. With deep thoughts I sleep until Saturday evening in infinite silence.

Even now, in the rented apartment not far from the university campus where I study philosophy, I can't fall asleep. My head is resting on my arm in the quiet kitchen. My wide eyes are looking for a way to get rid of the acute pain in my stomach that has been accosting me non-stop for days, especially at night. I open the fridge, drink some natural liquid laxative and sip a glass of water. I go to the bathroom and come back. The fridge door opens and closes again.

Reality awaits outside. I leave the house with a quick sandwich. I drive the white Camry and go down to the gas station by the sea, not far from the boardwalk, until I come to a stop. I ask them to fill 'er up, and walk towards the small coffee shop inside the station to get a cola in a glass bottle.

Some people have cigarettes or chewing gum. I have cola. The brand doesn't matter, as long as it's black and carbonated. I am addicted to the dissonance between the relaxed style of sipping small sips from the bottle, feeling the glass touching my lips, and the restlessness of the gas particles looking for a place to escape. I'm addicted to their plight.

A gas station by the beach is a moment of quiet. Warmth. Humidity. Taking a small sip, standing in the doorway between the restaurant and the sidewalk. Two old silver motorbikes with leather bags on their sides approach the station, probably to be filled up. Two men in their sixties, or a little over, are riding them. Half light blue and half light green helmets. Talking, they slowly glide into the station. They shout lightly to each other and, in the meantime, they pay and stick the fuel nozzle into the small silver tank.

"Amazing time we made today. What a trip, huh?" says one of them to the other. "What about Moses? Not coming anymore?"

"No," his colleague replies. "His new girlfriend, Bella, doesn't want to hear of it, and he listens to her. Can you believe it? He's stopped being a man. Lost his balls to the woman, don't you see? She sets limits for him. She's afraid. Says we go too fast. He must put her in her place."

Just as I start to cross the narrow road between the restaurant and the station, one of the riders starts driving. He jerks forward, bumping into me, stunned. Shards of the cola bottle fly into my eyes, dancing with the sea breeze. I have a small pouch, kind of a long pocket with a zipper and a clasp, that's usually wrapped around my waist, but a second ago I was holding it in my hands. It flew onto the road half open. Its contents are scattered on the pavement, next to the shattered Coke bottle that oozes black blood.

I lean into the road, together with the biker whose bag also flew and scattered its contents. An older man who offers a feeble apology while also bending down to pick up his stuff.

"Everything flew all over the place, gee," he complains with a frown.

I recognize a battered package that looks like medicine whose pills are strewn on the road, parts of a catheter and also an open wallet with some coins.

"What a mess," we both say and try to pick up the remains.

"OK, nothing bad happened," he says. "Can I make it up to you with a cup of coffee? Or the Coke you spilled? You know. Leviticus said an eye for an eye," the man says and hands me the pouch. "I'm sorry. It's yours, isn't it?" For a moment I'm gripped by a chill. I take the bag from him, arrange the bills and things in it, shove them deep inside and close it. As if the bag were a rare animal that someone is holding by the tail, causing it great discomfort.

Why is he talking about Leviticus?

"Excuse me?"

"You know, Leviticus says that if you do something bad, like hurt a person, you have to give them compensation."

I look at the floor and see the scattered caplets. The name of the product is written on the box: *Calm Blood Balm*. And in smaller letters: *Natural plant-based Caplets to relieve high blood pressure*. I collect as many as I can, put them in the box and hand it back to the older man. A quick glance at the clock shows I'm late. The tank is full. The older men get on the old bikes and resume their journey. I leave some bills at the gas station and drive away.

Chapter 9

On my second morning in the small apartment in Tenerife I wake up sweaty. A little shaky. It turns out I had slept for a long time, wandering between memory and oblivion. Between closed blinds in the light and an open window at night. An invisible force, that uncontrollable impulse that directed me like an arrowhead to this island, makes me decide that I must get out. That's it. This restlessness must be channeled elsewhere. It was as if the heat and burning plaguing me only motivated me further.

After thirty hours of sleep, I step into the shower. Boiling water flows over my body. Gradually, I increase the intensity of the heat. Set myself on fire, in a little cauldron of hell. I immerse myself in the water, with no notion of time.

I dress warmly. I take a pain reliever. Once in the small car I ask the navigator to show me the way to Cruz del Carmen, one of the places marked on my list of potential trips to the north of the island. I feel that the road speeds up for me, but I make an effort to stay within the speed limit. In the middle of the road, a phone call again. I silence it once more. The number shows it is one of the clients. Now I give myself over even more to the roads up the mountain which are unfamiliar to me. I need to be careful. After about an hour, I park the car outside the visitors center at the heights of the Anaga Rural Park, in the Macizo de Anaga, Tenerife's northern mountain range.

I park near a house of worship. "For hundreds of years we have been camping here to receive the prayer for the road, formulated three hundred years ago for those who walk on it," says a tour guide in English. "The blessing is in the name of the Virgen del Carmen. Carmen, the patron saint of Carmel, secluded herself in the mountain near Haifa in the Holy Land in the twelfth century. I can understand the Spaniards who came here. There really is something in this place reminiscent of those surroundings."

I hope so hard that the blessing reaches me too. Forget religion, after all, we are all children of God. I pass the stone-built restaurant. I stroll between the trees and immediately feel as if I had passed through a door into another space. A space with cool weather where the trees cradle the tranquility of the place and its high energy. A dense, tangled space that embraces and envelops me.

The laws of science are clear. The breathing of a person going down a road, exerting themselves—should be faster and more labored than usual. And so I set off, full power ahead. Even rage. But the path cares for me like a compassionate nurse: tree after tree merges into a forest of wonders, dense with intertwining ferns.

Logs laid horizontally serve as steps downhill. More and more stairs slow my stride. Each at a different distance and interval, forcing me to examine each one and plan the descent; to stop for a moment before continuing onwards; to breathe deeply while moving. The subtropical moss and a steep path strides me. The moist soil also makes me moderate my pace. I'm mostly alone. Hikers pass me by here and there. I walk past a cave and more lush vegetation. I inhale a concoction of air with an aroma to which I don't know how to assign a taste or a smell.

Almost an hour goes by until I cross a facility that looks like a water supply station, near a collection of bright houses. The path goes right through their yards. Not far from there are the plowed furrows of small fields. I read the name of the village on the sign: *Casa del Rio*. Using hand gestures, I ask one of the residents where the path continues. "Pah-tah-tah," he says, pointing towards the field. There were cabbages blooming next to the houses.

Gradually, the rainforests give way to a more open space, full of forest trees, which blends into and overlaps with the landscape. A group of forest rangers is working around some trees, forging pathways. I inquire about the name of the tree. "Wintigo," one of them tells me with a smile on his face. "Only in the Canary Islands." A spectacular native species of trees with leaves that turn red. The chirping birds are also hard to miss.

This is a trail whose path is unpredictable. The tapping of feet interferes with the rhythm, ruining any chance of keeping a tempo. Only concentrating and dealing with the constant change in the texture of the route. Another hour elapses, and I intersperse between the sides of the mountain and small terraces enclosed in mounds of earth that have been shaded to take advantage of any available space.

A sudden bend in the road hides a single house and its livestock: chickens, goats, a dog that follows me, a few small vineyards, juniper trees. Another small village that looks almost abandoned. Here and there new tenants are beginning to appear in the flora. Squatting in our hearts and accustoming our eyes. Fleshy cacti that keep multiplying. Dragon trees that get their haircuts at the salons of top stylists. After another fork, the sea comes into view again. Distant terraces, tight paths that descend even farther.

At an altitude of nearly 2,000 feet, the lowest point on the route before the ascent back, I sit down on a ground ledge and observe. In the distance, a lighthouse and the sea. Above it are several large rocks and, above them, the winding road. Between the mountains, in the rocks, one can see man-made ravines. Caves left by the Guanches, the island's earliest settlers. They dug them to protect themselves from heavy rains. Later, other settlers chose to build their homes on the mountain. To carve them out of the rocks. Thus the local village architecture was created.

Quite a few people tell me they go to the sea to relax. At the next viewpoint called Chinamada, I'm not on the beach but overlooking a strip of waves bounded by the edges of magnificent mountains. There is something in that blue that moves in such Escherian[1] motions, creating an unresolved illusory image.

I stay there dreaming for a long time. Listening to the quiet noise. The thin, micron-thick noise that tiny dogs might pick up on. I feel a touch away from something I don't know how to define and can't name. It has an element of melancholy, maybe a sour flavor.

One day, while Lake was sick in the hospital, I ran into an acquaintance who travels a lot. She told me that when things get tough, she takes a walk in nature. "Plants may not have a nervous system," she said, hanging her big, burning eyes on me, "but they respond. They have surviv-

---

1   As in Maurits Cornelis Escher

al reflexes, like releasing poison when they're eaten. There is communication between plants, even when they are far apart. I think we know almost nothing about them. I think that the colors, smells and movements of plants—they all make up a more delicate and complex language than that of humans. Do you get me? Nature simply expresses itself better than we do. It has many more colors in its palette."

After Lake passed away, she wrote me a message. "It's okay if you feel like running away. If life gives you lemonade, make some lemons."

"Don't you mean it the other way around?" I replied.

"No. I meant exactly what I said. You have lemonade right now—a concentrate with lots of water, rich, packed, overwhelming. You have to distance yourself a bit to feel the lemon. To exhaust the sourness. So that you can go back to enjoying drinking the lemonade.

Chapter 10

The route I take back from Chinamada is the so-called Lollipop Trail. If I want to make it to the end by daylight, it's time to leave. Therefore, I climb back along the same way I came down, taking a small but challenging detour.

In a path that skips and climbs up the road, the forest of ferns and laurel leaves reveals itself before me again. This time the feeling is a little different. The time on the trail may have done its job, and perhaps some layers of cynicism were peeled off of me. It is like watching a movie for the second time. How did I not see the stem growing at an impossible angle? How did I not notice the little nook hiding at the bend? The thin, shapely trees, as if they'd been frozen while parading on the catwalk in a fashion show, each caught in a different pose. One extending a flamboyant branch upwards. Another one spreading its branches in many shades of green. A third one branching in two.

In one of the directions there is a white house with a small yard. Tiny beds of vegetables, a fruit tree I don't recognize. The view and the surroundings inspire me. A little girl is playing hopscotch. As she jumps, she recites the numbers in Spanish. Her dress has a floral pattern, her braids are flying and her eyes are sweet. I breathe deeply and picture myself living there. It could be so complete, I muse. I will find a job I can do remotely. I will pay someone here to maintain my vegetable garden. How much can it cost? I picture myself writing, drawing and playing music.

"What are you talking about?" the voice in my head says immediately. Everything seems wonderful until you need milk, or until there's a power outage in the middle of the night, or you have a heart attack. And it's all in Spanish, of course. "It's not such a big deal," another voice counters. The supermarket is down there, only half an hour away, and today this place has all the infrastructure. And, in general, I'm as healthy as an ox, with a resting heart rate that's close to this girl's. No need to kill me ahead of time.

I get a little closer to the house, curious to see more: what a house like this looks like, what an environment like this is like. Out of the corner of my eye I see that on the other side there is an exit to the garden. The little girl approaches me. She has no anger or suspicion. On the contrary. She says something in Spanish that I don't understand. A mixture of words that describes something, judging by the movement of her hands.

When I look at the hopscotch drawn on the concrete, I see that it is very elaborate. Ornate. Full of colors and beautiful shapes. And not just simple ones, rather, there is an illusion of movement, as if something there in the concrete were moving through the beautiful colors. "Bravo," I say to her, clapping my hands. "Gracias, gracias," she says, bowing with a smile, lifting one side of her dress with one hand, as is customary when curtsying.

She goes on chatting with me in Spanish, while I struggle to understand. I stretch the boundaries of language. She describes something and I manage to catch the words:

"La casa esta de venta." Casa is home, I know. I know the word venta from another expression, so I assume the house is for sale. That already sounds like much more than a mere coincidence to me. I decide to have fun, or at least to tell myself I'm having fun and knock on the door. To check out the Casa and the Venta, wherever it may be.

A very nice woman who greets me with a big smile is standing by the door. She's also wearing a long light colored dress with small flowers.

"Casa de venta?" I ask and add some words to stress the fact that I only speak English. She touches me lightly, directing me to enter the house, which looks warm and cozy. In fact, she practically dances her way through the space. Her movements are fluid, gazellic. The blue square floor tiles are delimited by the white grout between them. The walls are white. The large room has wooden furniture and a modest kitchen. Without talking too much she directs me to the bathroom, to a small shower. The names of the rooms that come out of her mouth sound like poetry to my ears. "El baño, la ducha."

The yard is charming and overlooks an extraordinary view. It has a laundry room and a place to hang the clothes to dry. Explaining something in Spanish, the woman leads me through the yard to some service buildings where I notice a small tractor, various tools and even a pile of fodder, probably for the owner's horse. Suddenly she makes a joke, rolls with laughter, throws some straw in the air and some of it lands on both of us.

"How much do you want for the house?" I ask in English. To overcome the language gap and avoid any misunderstandings, she writes me a number on a sheet of paper she found inside the house.

Casa—50,000 Euros. Casa + Terreno—100,000 Euros.
"Okay," I say, "momento."

Is this true? I think to myself and compare it to real estate prices in my city. Not a crazy amount. It might just be possible. I'm even excited. With a hundred thousand euros I can buy my peace? Every morning by this magic forest? The sea view? The infinite silence carried by the wind?

I go out into the yard, raising my voice a little to make sure the lady understands that I need a moment. So what do I do now? Do I take down her contact details? Or call someone to consult with them? But whom? Mothers say that one should have friends who are doctors and lawyers, but they ever say anything about real estate agents in Tenerife. I do not give up. I have always taken chances in life, and this is such a moment. I take the lady's number, ask a few questions and everything else I need to stay in touch with her.

I'm back in the front yard. The colorful, swirling hopscotch is still going on. There's a feeling of celebration in the air. I'm calm and optimistic. I come closer to the girl and slowly coordinate the jumps with her. I'm actually not bad at it. Hop, jump from square to square while every square moves. The colors of the chalk smear, bounce, run and splatter everywhere, which is really fun. It's fun to loosen up. My movements become more and more dance-like, and so do the little girl's. I sing Skew by Eefje de Visser, in Dutch. We move in waves, like divers whose sea is the mountain air. We float among the fish in the air. My bag grows wings, the dry fit top expands into a fluttering dress.

The girl joins in, mimicking me without understanding

the words, just as I didn't understand them when I first heard the song. And so we, in the small village of Río del Sol, on the main Cruz del Carmen road, in the heart of the rainforest mountains of the Anaga Rural Park, dance for a long time. Jumping and syncing our movements like a couple of professional dancers.

At the height of the dance I jump to the edge of the court, swinging a long leg forward. My foot gets caught in a tree root, one of many scattered in the forest jutting above the surface. My ankle is twisted for a moment, and the next, my body teeters at about three inches from the ground, then sways forward, until I end up lying flat on the ground.

I'm dazed and blurred by the forced landing. My wrist hurts from the crash. My knee is pretty shaken, but overall I'm fine. It takes me a few seconds to recover and turn my head. The girl is not there. There is no hopscotch court drawn on the concrete. There is no garden. The house looks very run down. The door is closed, locked and bolted.

I get up and smooth out my clothes, rearrange my bag and start walking with a slight limp about half a mile to the finish line. Disappointed. Confused. The fall brings me back to reality, and yet I still have a need to recreate my experience of this morning, the feeling of the forest of wonders that I tasted, even if briefly.

On the way back to El Suculum I keep thinking about this feeling. I once read about something called the Reward Circuit. The frontal cortex and the amygdala are responsible for the process of us wanting something increasingly more—for our addictions. In the past, it was called the Pleasure Center. This path is hidden deep in the brain, in a part that was created perhaps five hundred million years ago. It is interwoven with the parts responsible for our behavior and feelings such as hunger, thirst and sexual desire.

No one is worse than me, the king of control. I can't let go. No one keeps things in order like I do. So strictly. The dishes, the grocery shopping. Not too much dancing either. No kidding around. No drinking. No addictions. Planning properly before saying anything. Weighing each word. Juggling with letters. Delivering taglines. I always said to myself, look at all these politicians, businessmen and opinion leaders. They're addicts. They take huge risks for their passions. Just to sniff a little more power or money or any other feeling. What a tragedy. Some of them also fall, precisely because of this. From the excess publicity and adulation, they get divorced and end up living in terrible loneliness. Some of them, because of the financial power they possess, get involved in affairs with escort girls.

One sunny day, the computer system of one of my clients, a large academic institution, was hacked. The person responsible, it turned out, was the finance director who had resigned only a short time earlier. None of the police detectives came up with the solution, not even a private investigator. It was a retiree with a heavy Indian accent who worked for the CFO as a bookkeeper who shed light on the case. That morning she entered the computer room and scanned it with her experienced, senior eyes. She looked everywhere. She saw the empty coffee cup with the black, muddy remains. The forgotten reading glasses and newspaper. She then felt the screens, looked from side to side and squatted down. Frowning, she noticed some crumbs on the floor. She picked up a few of them, smelled them and examined them in depth.

He liked cheap croissants that came half-frozen, half-baked from the Valley Bakery. That's what she said in her testimony. He used to warm them in the toaster oven. They would turn out fresh and a little crispy, the way he liked them.

"These croissants are mind-altering substances," he used to say. "They wrote with me the best wording for our financial statements."

"I also had an addiction," said the bookkeeper. "I have worked in many jobs throughout my career, and I always brought my home-made sweets to the office. It was my addiction. Feeling the ingredients in your hands, absorbing heat from the pan. To watch people eating and enjoying them. I also knew how to bake croissants myself. But he, in my last workplace before retirement, he of all people, couldn't stand my home-made pastry, and preferred this terrible vacuum-packed kind."

It should be mentioned that she received a reward for making the discovery, as this addiction was fertile ground to reveal his embezzlement of funds and even sexual harassment. When she came to offer me her condolences for Lake, she told me that she now spends half of her time in Rishikesh and practices meditation regularly.

Meditation. There are also good addictions. But if I've come this far, why am I so scared of letting myself live here and indulge in the feeling I experienced in the Forest of Wonders? You consume too much psychedelic rock and literature on the Woodstock culture, says the voice in my head, explaining that we will have to wean ourselves off that too. Come out of your naivety, he adds. Grow up and grow better. This is not the right direction. The landscape neither releases nor appeases.

I answer that I am falling into my own trap. I didn't come all this way to think the same way I thought before. What is the point of repeating the same experiment twice and expecting a different result? Let it go, because I may have inhaled my own drug now. This path, deep in the forest, is so deeply hidden. As deep as that moment when you allow yourself to scream a silly summer hit in the car when no one is listening. Maybe you need to run really far away to give your drug a place to live within you. Or maybe this is the good addiction I need right now in order to stop and leave everything I want to leave behind? Here, in a place where no one hears and the trees ingest everything, enveloping you in green, brown and gray.

I am now standing on the roof of my guest house overlooking the sunset and the slopes of the mountain crowned with cacti. The cell phone is buzzing. It's the office again. I silence the device but am tempted to look at the messages. There are many of them. The partner looked for me numerous times. I don't answer him. I don't. Time and time again.

But one missed call in particular catches my attention. It's from God. And there's a message. Get in touch with us. You still haven't taken care of what needs to be done. I need to talk to you anyway. I debate whether to text him back. It's God, after all. With everything else, the office can manage for a day or two, or three. At worst, we might lose a client. But God?

I start looking for his number in my favorite contacts. I hold my cell phone closer, then farther away from me, then decide to put it aside. It seems like betrayal to me. I didn't come here in order to return his calls. I have to give myself another chance. To take another step forward. To not get back to the safe haven of the office. On the contrary. To increase the dose, to taste more. Maybe this is what is needed. Maybe my future is here, in the air of Tenerife. Maybe everything is simply here, in this all-inclusive deal, including the peace and tranquility.

Chapter 11

The Funeral

On a particularly hot day about twenty years ago, on the outskirts of town, a half-broken gate made of stone opened into a paved path. A few dozen people were standing there. They seemed a little lost. Some of them exchanged ideas on how to find a kerchief or part of a garment to protect them in tough times.

Opposite us was the sea. Dazzlingly shiny. At 5:00 pm it was still hot. "I came straight from the office," said a half-bent man to his friend who got out of a rusty, battered van. "I didn't get the details. I understand it was a heart attack. How old was he?"

The friend scratched his unkept beard. Gathering his shirt in a spin, he tucked the hem in under the crotch. "He wasn't even sixty. Who dies at that age today?" Both of them strode through the gate with the important air of prime ministers, in complete dissonance to the ragged shoes and white shirt with ketchup stains, a result of eating lots of hamburgers on the road, especially in the center of town.

I stood there on the side. The son of the deceased. In jeans one size too big, flared at the bottom. Heavy brown work boots. A baseball cap on my head. I walked slowly into the crowd, until I was swallowed up, silent in the river of mourners.

They entered the shaded area. "Where is the son? Let him come to stand next to me." The officiant began the ceremony. After two minutes I felt the soft pain of an elbow stabbing me. "What is this?" A short and extremely broad man standing next to me asked me in a whisper. "Who does he think he is, the Beatles? How long are the prayers and the sobbing going to be? Like Tony Bennett is here. Not at all authentic, not moving. Just replicating the previous funeral. Don't they pay him enough?"

The stretcher followed by the participants began its procession into the cemetery. About seven hundred feet away stood tents with bright red logos. People crowded under them. An impressive middle-aged woman stepped out of the crowd. My mother. She didn't scream, or howl. She simply described the deceased and exalted his former virtues.

My eyes absentmindedly scanned the surroundings until my gaze fell on a young woman standing under the rays of the sun. She wasn't wearing sunglasses, so I could make out her eyes. They were brown, round and very large. Almost like in cartoons. She wore a short black dress. Not a symbol of modesty in a cemetery.

"This one too. Orating like she's Abe Lincoln now. Sounds like plastic. Not touching at all," the overweight young man whispers in my ears again, not really caring about the fact that he's referring to my mother. I can't take my eyes off the young woman in the black dress. I notice a drop sliding down her face. It's flowing from the corner of her eye to the side of her nose and mouth, and from the neck down to the cleavage hidden in her dress. I follow the drop with my eyes, unsure of whether it is a tear or a bead of sweat. Then comes another one.

I get a little closer to get a better view, ignoring the officiant who steals a glance at me. A few minutes later, the Lord, his shepherd maketh him to lie down in green pastures, and leadeth him beside the still waters. He restoreth his soul too. The air actually cools down a little, and the blowing sea breeze mixes a strong cocktail of sea salt, humidity and sounds from the nearby shopping mall.

Then another drop trickles down. A little moisture, slim, clearing a trail along a lightly made-up face, down the small part of the angle of the jaw. A face slightly flushed from the heavy heat. Leaving a trail that bears witness like a thousand witnesses. The teardrop slowly continues its way along the line of the black dress. My gaze is fixed on the same line that clearly bears witness to the fact that there is no bra there. Only a drop disappearing into the skin, and it's anyone's guess where it may end up.

I was handed the microphone. All that came out of my mouth was a painfully loud feedback screech. I said I couldn't speak because I was sad. My robotic eyes fixed on the air and locked. My voice disappeared. The impressive woman passed the microphone to the young broad man.

"His son is here with us, but we too have lost a father," he began with a cliché and added a tremor to his voice. "We didn't sell gummies or sea balls. We sold people joie-de-vivre, hope and happiness." Suddenly there was a scream. Or rather, a groan, coming from the other end of the gathering up the road, interrupting the young man's flowing speech.

A teen girl had crashed into the woman in the black dress now leaning on the fence by the wash basin, knocking her off with her bike, and then falling to the ground herself. She cried, and asked for forgiveness, stammering that she hadn't been able to hit the brakes on time.

"Jonah always championed this concept," the fat young man continued, "either you do something with all your heart, or better don't do it at all."

This is where something was supposed to happen. For example: *I approach the young woman with a chivalrous smile, acting as the perfect gentleman. She falls in love with me in an instant. We go to a movie or a stroll on the boardwalk.*

But none of that happened. I just stood there. Stuck like the marble on a grave.

One man, another employee of the store, helped the beautiful young woman pull herself together a bit. Asked if she was okay and if there was anything he could do to help, making every effort to get things back on track. With a light movement of his hand he picked up the girl's bike and the girl herself. Wordlessly he sent her on her way. For a moment it looked like he was shrinking, like in the story of Alice in Wonderland.

"Not many know that Jonah employed so many people. It wasn't just the store. It wasn't just the branch in Midtown or at the bayside, open 24/7 all year round." The cynical chubby man with the ketchup stains on his shirt had a hard time holding back the tears of true friendship flowing down his cheeks. I had to turn away, hoping no one saw the tears running down my cheeks. The truth is that it happens to me recently sometimes. This whole feelings thing. I can't understand why I suddenly burst into tears after some song. Crying so hard that I have to stop the car on the side of the road and take a moment to calm down. Back in the day, my dad offered me all kinds of advice. He explained to me that business should not involve emotions. The four-beat method for example—hold your breath for four seconds, exhale for four seconds, inhale for four seconds and close by exhaling for another four seconds.

"Jonah," the fat man tried to get back to where he was, "read the terrain. He knew the little details and always surprised us. I am convinced that after his death we will find out even more about the amazing person he was. And perhaps some things we will never know." The fat man now turned his gaze towards the sea. The sun was setting in the outskirts of the town. Suddenly there was silence. The hundreds who came to the gates of the cemetery became quiet. For a moment it looked like a commercial for a condo by the sea or for relaxing at the end of the day with a glass of whiskey.

The fat man was replaced by the man with the unkept beard. "Silent as the grave here, huh?" He said in a loud voice, and all at once the crying and tears subsided. Some people giggled, others smiled awkwardly. For some reason, no one was outraged by the lack of tact. "It's okay, everyone. Those of our employees who need to, may take a day or two off to pull themselves together and come back next week as good as new. We've left some refreshments up by the entrance. We invite you to the canopy to exchange a few words, and then everyone will go their separate ways and we will figure out how to proceed from now on."

The bearded and the fat man strode with determination and excessive confidence. After them, the others flowed slowly, placing flowers on the tomb, then ascended like a swarm of buzzing bees to the refreshment area.

All the clichés were placed one after the other on the disposable plastic plates under the canopy. I could see the packaging. This is where their bodies are laid out, just before they are buried together in brown plastic. Simple corpses, unbranded. Without a father or a mother. After all, Dad had started out selling Nestle, Kellogg's, Frito-Lay.

One day, when I was twelve years old, I asked him: "Dad, how much do you earn when you sell Fritos?"

"Ten, twenty percent," he replied.

"No one in my class can tell the difference between Fritos and generic corn chips. Just give me the unbranded generic ones." That's all I said. Dad thought about it for a few weeks, then decided I was a genius and that he needed me at the store. I didn't understand his calculation tables, but within two months all the large corporations left his chain and were replaced by others. The ones that are here with us today. "Freetoes—spiced potato slices you'll tap into"; "Kinkat, never a dull bite"; "Mingles, the potato snack for singles."

I could never escape the voices in my head recounting phrases like those. I once had a friend who said it was funny how someone who couldn't stand even a little spice, certainly not the sharpest kind, was the spiciest, sharpest, most creative person she knew. And that was also my problem. That's exactly the reason why she left me. "You run away to literature, to the sharp side. And most certainly when you have to talk about feelings, definitely." Definitely. I remember her saying that word over and over again. Definitely her parents' divorce when she was only five weighed heavily on her and came out in every sentence she said.

I walked around between the plates for a bit, but didn't eat anything. People spoke. Some of them still had the signs of crying on their faces. Others were just chatting or joking. The beautiful young woman was no longer there. It was weird but maybe she just dropped by for a moment. Her skin, between light and dark, but especially her brown eyes. Eyes that seem to express everything that goes on inside or in the world in general. They didn't leave my mind. And it even surprised me, as a fan of medium-size boobs—which is exactly what she had there. Why the eyes and not the boobs?

Turns out we're worth something, after all, said the narrator who's always inside my mind. The one who, despite himself, sometimes emerges without me noticing.

My legs hurt. I don't get this either. It's not like I had been there that long, but still. I had a terrible sensation in my legs. Mainly on my feet. I sat down on a plastic chair next to one of the refreshment stands, then leaned back, not very comfortably. Not far from there, actually really close but completely behind me, stood the fat man and the bearded one. Dad's two partners.

I cocked my head slightly to sharpen the hearing in one of my ears without them realizing I was listening.

"Listen. One minute on daily matters, if you don't mind," the fat man spoke, clearly worried, but in a calm voice. "The $4.90 candy is completely sold out, and the cartons aren't coming in. Too bad, we're losing a ton of dough. What do we do with this supplier, Carlos? He keeps disappearing and then tells me some story about his trucks being delayed by extra inspections when crossing the border. Extra inspections my ass."

"Right. They're very profitable," replied the bearded man. "Maybe I'll ask Nate. He's for all-local workers. He must have a proper supplier. After all, he brought us a wonderful container full of balloons this year for the 4th of July, the ones with the stars that glow in the dark. We made about 150,000 on that one alone."

The two went on talking as if they were at the office and not in the middle of a funeral ceremony. Until a lady, one quite advanced in age, approached the broad man and said: "I used to be your customer for years. I used to buy popsicles for my son at your Midtown store. And now for my grandson too. Tell me. How did you manage to bring in all this shade, the canopies, the refreshments. Is it allowed?"

The fat man looked at her with kind eyes, but nevertheless those of a shrewd merchant. "You're right. It's a bit forbidden, but we work regularly with the administrator of the cemetery. He has a tab with us at the store, and allowed us this as a one-off."

The woman tightened her face for a moment as if a smile was about to spread over it, but then it turned into a frown, almost like she was about to cry. She looked at both of them. Without words. "One-off," the bearded man repeated, breaking the silence. "Maybe you need help getting home. Would you like one of our employees to drive you?"

The caresses of the wind. From the chair one could see the sun had already dipped into the sea. I noticed the lady's deep gaze, and again tears appeared in my eyes. Not only that. I also felt something on my forearm, not far from the elbow, brushing against me; touching and not quite touching. Tickling. As a loving woman sometimes does.

"I'm fine," the woman tried to justify her reaction. "It's just that my husband is in a hospice, and I thought, when the time comes. Soon. We too might need something like that."

As though the most tactless sentence in the world hadn't been uttered, the fat and bearded men didn't seem the least bit uncomfortable. "We will arrange something for you," the bearded man said in a soft voice. "Here's my card." He patted several places on his body, pulled out a rather crumpled card, then apologized and reached into his pockets again, giving her another business card, equally crumpled.

And again the pleasant wind and the feeling of the light touch took hold of me. A close sense of connection between strangers. The feeling of basic human kindness in every person.

"Thanks. What does it say here? I can't make it out. It says Lucky Bail and then there's this black ink stain," she says, fixing her gaze on the card.

"Ah... no, it's nothing. It's Lucky Bailey. The "ey" doesn't show, because there's a permanent stain on all the cards. But we got ten cents off on each one. Smart move, wasn't it?"

"Jonah & Sons," the woman called out loudly and then repeated it again, this time with a question mark.

"'Jonah & Sons?' I didn't know he had sons. Are they here? Maybe I'll offer them my condolences."

"No. Not sons. Only one son. He had no family," the fat man said one of the weirdest things. And sons. Neither his son nor his wife. The lady turned to me and shook my hand.

"I'm sorry for your loss." The bearded man escorted the lady to where my mom stood and waited in silence. The lady spoke to her and then the bearded man walked her to the car of one of the employees.

I turned my gaze back and found out that the pleasant tickling came from the disposable white plastic tablecloth set between the cheap refreshments and the stinging, disposable folding table. A white tablecloth whose edge, with a large, dry stain from being washed in ketchup, touches it and breaks off. Touches it and detaches.

Chapter 12

Let's bring it out into the open. So, like today, funerals and periods of mourning are excellent times to renew ties. One winter day I was with a colleague on our way to a meeting with a potential client. Or, to be precise, she was dragging me to a meeting with a potential client almost by force.

This was a colleague who once worked in the public relations department of our office. After I left for a new workplace, we continued to maintain a friendly relationship, which also included business collaborations with clients and mutual professional assistance. We hadn't seen each other in two years nor had we been able to do any business together. When Lake passed away she came to offer her condolences and, a few months later, she begged me to go with her to see a potential client.

"We're completely stuck in traffic. And, if we arrive, we will be spectacularly late," we both said into the interior of the car, over the loud pounding of the rain which at times turned into hail.

"It's fine," said the potential client on the other side. "Let's put it on the dashboard, where the bobble-head dog sometimes sits." I wished he had canceled the meeting, but my colleague insisted.

We started with a professional conversation in preparation for our presentation. The temperature dropped even lower. Heavy rain flooded the underpass, paying off promissory notes of drainage canals and rivers. We found ourselves in the midst of the deluge, while pandemonium broke out. We made slow progress, brainstorming for ideas and crawling along the highway.

"Can I change the subject for a moment?" she said to me after a while and went on speaking, without waiting for my answer. "After my divorce, my ex-husband fell ill and declared bankruptcy, and my daughter went through a difficult period. You probably remember all this. I told you that I would sometimes wake up at ten in the morning with no energy, dragging myself through another day, trying to take care of some freelance clients after I was fired from that office. I was in a very bad place."

"Sure, I remember."

"So one day I started to work at a clinic that treated children with anxiety, learning disabilities, they performed tests, etc. You can imagine how my number of clients had been dwindling. I had neglected them. I wasn't answering their calls. I curled up in bed and then made up all kinds of excuses like I was very busy with lots of non-existent projects. Then an old acquaintance brought their child to the clinic to consult with a test anxiety specialist. He told the owner about my background and recommended she hire me as her PR agent. I remember the job interview very well, the questions I was asked, the answers I gave. It started as a normal work conversation about branding needs and what features should be promoted to the media, and then about my knowledge and experience.

During the conversation about business experience, while I sat comfortably in the armchair, feeling more relaxed, sipping coffee, her questions became more personal. A conversation about 'do you know this and that person...' and then it shifted towards really personal matters. She talked about herself, I about myself, and whoop – we were there.

"She is a professional, a therapist. She recognized exactly where I was in life. After an hour and a half, she said jokingly that she wouldn't charge me for a double session, but would be willing to start working with me only if I now sat in the room and wrote down ten things in my life that gave me moments of happiness."

"OK." The rain outside abated a little. The cars stood almost motionless one behind the other waiting for salvation to come from heaven. Or from the traffic police.

"You know me. I am very frank. I say what I think. It has cost me several clients who left me. At first I resisted, aggressively. I told her I was there as a PR professional. I even raised my voice. But she insisted, answering me firmly. Eventually she got up, said she was going to the bathroom for a moment and then closed the door behind her and said loudly from the other side of the door that she would be back in an hour and expected to see a start by then. At least two or three things.

"'What?' I shouted, banging on the door. I told her she couldn't do that. Then I looked at the room around me, sat back down, and took a sip of water. Anything to avoid doing it. In the end I decided to write something just to get it out of the way. I needed money like air to breathe. After pondering for a bit, I took a pencil and wrote down on the paper in front of me: the moment my daughter hugged me the night before. The slalom I ran with a hard-boiled egg in the kitchen that looked like an episode from a sitcom, a kind word another client said to me a week before, after I arranged a TV interview for him."

"I get it," I said, "alright."

"Two weeks later we sat down to do some work and, at the end of the meeting, she again made the continuation contingent on me writing the list. This time it was easier, and I was a little more willing to cooperate. After all, I could already see my professional fee at the end of the tunnel. A month later, she suggested I keep a happiness diary—a log of the good, special moments in your past or present."

"Nothing does me any good," I answered her bitterly. "I get up on auto mode. Sometimes I don't even get up at all. Neither in auto mode nor any other way."

"I know. I also felt that way for a long time. I suggest you try. Start small and see where it goes. I survived thanks to my journal. I would be happy to show it to you."

"I'll show you mine if you show me yours," I joked sorely, cutting through the waves like a sailboat, exiting the expressway. "I go to the office and the papers in front of me confuse me. I'm on the computer and get angry about everything. I go shopping at a pharmacy and start crying because there is an adult diaper section. All I want is to get back to bed. At least it's warm there. Or here, in the car. With all the rain, the heating works wonderfully in here."

"I understand. I honestly understand. Still, give me two moments that have been good for you lately," she says. She's trading with me in the market of positive psychology.

"Honestly. It's awkward for me," I reply to her, trying to keep my cool. "Leave me alone."

We are surfing in a puddle. The rain is now hitting the

windshield and the roof hard. We are near the parking lot adjacent to the client's office. Cars and spots corralled in a game of cat and mouse. Waiting for someone to leave so someone can glide in. The parking spots are taken. The cars lie in ambush waiting for their prey. So do we. I sniff around like an experienced hunter looking for tracks. Who is running to their car with an umbrella, who turned on the front lights for a moment and is maybe about to start the car and leave. I notice a distant spot at the end of the row. I roll towards it, approaching cautiously. Suddenly, another vehicle speeds past us, makes a huge wave in the puddle and then swerves for some unknown reason. I hold on to the steering wheel for dear life, trying not to get hit and also trying not to lose the free spot, until I manage to dodge him at the last minute by driving through the deep side of a puddle on the edge of the lot.

I open the window for a moment, catching a shower of rain on my head. My door is next to a concrete hemisphere on the curb that's blocking any possibility of me opening it enough to get out. On the other side, a car is parked right next to the white separation line.

"I can only get out on your side," I say to my colleague. "I don't have an umbrella. Can you hold it open while I climb out?"

"I will get out, open the door for you and even stand in the rain for you," she says, "provided you tell me two good things that happened to you recently. Two moments of happiness."

"This isn't the time for games. We're super late," I try to mitigate the evil of her decree, but to no avail. She insists, waves her umbrella and even opens the door for a moment to prove to me the seriousness of her intentions.

"Okay, okay." I surrender. "Give me a moment to think."

We're sitting in the heated car. I lean my head back. straining my memory. Trying to dredge up such a moment. "Dinner with a couple of my childhood friends and their kids a few days ago. I was able to ignore everything on my mind. The children talked about their day. My friends talked about their memories. Is that good enough for you? Does it meet the criteria?" I say with all the cynicism I can muster to get her off my back.

"Way to go!" she returns the barb. "You really did great. Now one more."

I kept silent. Glanced around. Studied my keys, the display, the speedometer. My mobile phone, my glasses. I was looking for tracks of myself, for myself. I glazed at the back seat, reached out and pulled out a bag. "This. This bag."

"Is this bag a moment of happiness?" She smiles and then laughs. "What's in there? To me a bag of happiness is gummy snakes, popsicles and some sour candies. I know it's worse than petrol, but it's my happiness."

"There's no candy in there," I say. "I had to clean out the stuff from the nightstand next to his bed. Medications, some bandages. It was really hard for me to see parts of pill packets, eye drops. Like sticking your hands in thorns."

"Listen," she stops me in the middle. "You're going against the rules. Moments of happiness only. Give me a happy moment."

"I'm getting there," I interrupt her. "I noticed that the dresser drawer wouldn't move. Something was getting in the way. I checked deep behind it, until I found something stuck at the bottom. It was a bag of black stopwatches. A bag he bought for the WCA Rubik's Cube competitions.

For a second, but only for one second, I had the feeling that Lake had sprung up and was about to distribute them among the participants. It was like a greeting from the past for me. I felt like an archaeologist who found a Julius Caesar coin or a medium who managed to communicate with a spirit."

She thought for a moment, then laid the umbrella on the floor of the car and caressed my cheek, which had a tear trickling down on it. "Okay, my friend," she said in a broken voice. "I'll make this one count for you." Game over.

Chapter 13

On the fifth morning of my stay in Tenerife I focus on attempting to translate my feelings and on the feasibility of living in this place. My methodology includes a small notepad and a pen left on the table, a gift from the owner of the B&B to their guests.

I collect evidence like the investigation team in an aviation disaster, trying to learn lessons. One should write down the price of tomatoes or apples compared to what they cost back home. The price of gas? Do they recycle here? Where are the nice neighborhoods? Is there any sort of community here that meets to participate in interesting activities? Along with this, I also record the moments of happiness, the sites of absorption that promote calmness. Like that moment in Anaga.

Simple math. A good fresh vegetable salad I like plus two eye drops from a local forest or mountain pharmacy to soothe the vision in my eyes. The ocean, in an exclusive edition, will bring my heartrate down. A breath of saline[2] will reduce the congestion in the lungs.

Like a serious professional, I also go for qualitative research. Wandering on foot around different neighborhoods, going into gas stations and supermarkets, coming

---

2   3 Salt solution

across people on the street and asking questions. "Excuse me ma'am, I was told there is a good running store here. Do you happen to know where it is?" I drop by a community center in another neighborhood of the city and, with the help of Google Translate, I try to figure out what classes they offer. I think to myself that I should learn Spanish, so that my Spanish repertoire doesn't consist only of a few words out of Julio Iglesias songs.

On the weekend I wander around the outskirts of the city. On one of the streets I come across a sign that says: *Casa y Café*, placed above a large interior space with brown wooden tables and chairs. On one side there is a coffee stand with drinks and pastries and, on the other, a real estate agency with pictures of houses and shops. I enter to check it out.

The skilled broker offers me coffee. I go to the cash register, order a vanilla green tea, pay with my cellphone and sit down. She introduces herself briefly, tells me a little about being the 'oldest real estate broker in the area' and adds that, since I am a foreigner, neither from the area nor from Spain, this is just the place for me. "We understand your needs."

Then she starts showing me pictures. A spectacular fashion show of exquisite homes that fulfill the American or Spanish dream, or any dream of someone from the European Union. And the logic is clear. No one wants to be where or what they are right now. We are all wannabe's. Everyone actually wants to feel a little more. Enjoy the fragrance of a slightly higher class. Therefore, show potential clients houses a little above what they can afford. To excite them. To arouse a liking. To get the heart hooked. And say sentences like: "It's only one point three million" or "only one and a half million, but it comes with a garden and a parking garage."

She directs me to an older woman, Clara, who actually has excellent, almost Oxfordian English. Clara is curious about me. She asks where I'm from. Why I am considering moving here and what interests me. I give her the minimum necessary details. I maintain the expression of a retired accountant. She remains silent. Smiling. She leaves for a moment and comes back with a cup of hot tea, which she sips slowly.

"You need a home, but not here. Farther south. Not in one of the big cities," she declares. "You need a house overlooking the ocean or the mountains, on the main road between the north and the south." Her determination sounds like a verdict being read out in a courtroom. "I have a few houses to show you in Araya, in Vilaflor. What do you think? Shall we arrange a short trip together?" She's polite but decisive. I do not argue. I tell myself that I can use the opportunity to have a guided tour, for now.

Right after the weekend, on Monday morning, we set off. As I expected, Clara is dressed in her Monday best, complete with a light, wide-brim hat on her head. While we drive, she occasionally drops some data about the demand for apartments according to their proximity to the city, altitude and remoteness, inasmuch as these factors can count on such a small island. Everything is determined by the throngs of foreigners who love to buy apartments close to the beach and entertainment areas.

A third of the way south of Santa Cruz she tells me to get off at the nearest interchange. We turn right and then left, then climb up the street and stop at a house with an orange facade. We walk towards the door that is up one flight of stairs from the courtyard. Clara unlocks it with the key.

Classic brown terracotta tiles, blue doors, a small living room, a kitchen with a range hood, one bedroom and a small balcony, ten by fifteen feet, overlooking the sea beyond the highway and some houses in the village.

She is waiting for me to wander, explore and take in the serenity and coolness of the house. We sit down on the cream-colored couch. "One thousand square feet. One hundred and thirty thousand euros. A house that has everything. Even furniture, if you want it." She doesn't wait for me to voice an opinion. "We can also help you with a mortgage. If you take half the value of the house as a mortgage, it will be about 1,300 euros per month."

Clara pushes me to the practical side of things. Electricity rates. The solar water heater in the apartment. She has all the answers ready. "The owner of the house built five buildings in a row here. There is a solar panel system on the roof. When he was looking for land to build on, he checked the distance from the supermarket and the sea and the recreation areas on the beach below. You have a supermarket very close by. ALDI. A fifteen minute drive."

I go out to the balcony. I'm trying to figure out what I think of this apartment. Looking at the mirror reflected from the window, at the adjacent neighbors and the cars passing by every few minutes. One neighbor has an argument with another. In the distance some tourists are laughing.

"Do you know that it's literally a few minutes' walk from the boardwalk and the beautiful anchorage you see there at the end?" Clara points out from inside the house. "Many people love going there. It's happy and pleasant, with shops, restaurants, a small fishing port, also a few pubs and clubs. Twice a week there is a lively market here, right at the end of the street. You have very nice neighbors on the floor above you and the house is adjacent to two other families. On one side is a sweet older couple and, on the other side, a young family who are away most of the time."

I linger for a moment. Trying to understand. If everything here is so useful and compact, what is bothering me? And is there a holding point for a moment of happiness? Can I imagine myself hanging out here, sleeping here? Everything is appropriately packaged here. I feel like I'm in a well-planned and laid out apartment, like in a Netflix series. An English-speaking community. I open the empty notebook of happiness. Before I write, I realize this is too canned. Too made-to-order. And maybe too serial. And perhaps 'lively' is actually more like 'noisy.'

Then I write TRANQUILITY in big letters. Across the entire page.

"Let's go on, Clara. Thanks. I'll consider it," I say and we are off to our next destination.

Chapter 14

We continue to the next houses. One after the other. My imaginary spreadsheet fills up with technical data. High or low. Spacious. Where the toilet is located. What the neighborhood is like. Whether there are many children around or it's rather an adult environment. Remote or close to all the action.

"This terrace is terrible," I say to her about one of the houses. "I'll spend most of my time cleaning." In another, I complain of strong winds. A narrow entrance. Rooms that are too small. Another house, spread over three stories—is way too big.

Two days go by. We see six more houses. Towards noon we drive down to the Playa de la Américas. It's got everything. A city full of tourists. Tens of thousands of hotel rooms and holiday apartments. "I can show you lots of great opportunities here as well. It is more suitable for those who want to buy a property as an investment. Five million people come here every year. At least one million of them, just for the beach. There are water sports, pubs, night clubs, and snooker. Do you like billiards? Golf? There is also a water park here. Will you be hosting children here? It's a great way for them to pass the time. And dolphins—multitudes of dolphins, you can watch them for hours. There are also shops for sale here, you can get a good deal. They buy everything here, the tourists, everything. There's a lot of spending going on here."

I suggest we eat lunch on the boardwalk. The weather here always seems to be warm and pleasant. Sunburned tourists wearing no shirts, girls in thin flip flops. The boardwalk is full of them, of all ages. Laughing and relaxed. We sit down to eat at a random restaurant on the waterfront.

"So, Clara. Tell something about yourself. So far I am the only one who has been answering questions here." I smile, trying to lighten the mood. I pour red wine into her glass and mine.

"Clara," she says as if starting a grocery list, "Casa y Café is a family business. Real estate, homes. Some businesses. My sister manages the Gran Canaria branch, the biggest one with the most transactions. Today her children also work in the business as agents. My brother's son is in Puerto Ventura. His poor father died when he was really young. You saw my daughter when you came to our office, she manages the Santa Cruz branch. She's also already bringing my grandchildren up to speed."

"Have you been doing this for a long time?" I try to express as much interest as possible after ordering my pasta from the waitress.

"We're one of the oldest. My parents opened the business after World War II. Foreigners have always been our best customers, but the residents of the Canaries also have to change apartments sometimes, right?"

"So the owner herself is showing me around? To what do I owe this honor?"

"You..." she hesitates for a moment and empties another glass. She seems to be used to drinking. "You are an interesting case," she stresses the last bit. "And I handle the special cases myself. It's a chance for me to take a trip in the sun, not sit in the office all day. To take some time off from my husband. To diversify. You must travel a lot." She returns the ball to my court.

"The truth is, not a whole lot. Most of our business is with local clients, although we also have a few abroad." I guess I had mentioned the office at some point. "If I travel, it's mostly on holidays."

"Is it a large office?" She sniffs some more.

"Pretty big. Big customers: ministers, companies, public figures, various organizations, institutions." She seems satisfied with the answer.

"And you?"

"What about me?"

"Do you travel a lot?"

"Relatively little. Sometimes to visit relatives. We have some in several corners of the globe. Our ancestors came from Spain, England and France. So you've been here all your life?"

"My whole life."

"How does it feel to live in a house that constantly has guests? Lots of guests, I mean." To encourage her to give me an honest answer, I add: "I am also asking as a potential resident in your country."

"I grew up like this. It really feels like we live in one big resort. You meet a lot of people from different nations."

She keeps to her European manners, while I try to extract something more genuine. To crack the conservative facade of the hat, the meticulous make-up, the good shoes and the chignon that never for a moment ceases to sell. "It's definitely interesting to meet people who come from all sorts of places," I say. "But still, these people—sometimes they don't have the best habits, you know."

"Yes," she sighs, "but still we work well together."

"We have a place like the Playa de la Américas," I try another angle. "It's called Blue Beach. Well, I'm exaggerating. Blue Beach is very small. The diversity there is different. But the principle is similar. I have friends there who say that it is very difficult to live in a city where you are constantly walking among strangers looking at you like you are in a zoo, and sometimes behaving wildly."

"It happens once in a while," she admits and, at last, I manage to find a small crack.

For a few minutes we concentrate on our dishes. She occasionally sips wine and I sip water.

"The sea is beautiful here," I say.

A light breeze moves the tablecloth. The pergola above gives us shade. For the first time I discern in Clara a smile that isn't only one of politeness. "The pasta we were served at this restaurant on the boardwalk is cooked in local sea water. We have a different sea. Our own sea."

I look at the ocean. It is not at all like the sea at home. The motion of the waves is more open compared to the high-wave aggressiveness of the North Atlantic. It is a different blue, in shades of grayish-green-turquoise and others that have no name. The horizon is also different. Maybe when you're in the Mediterranean, you pre-limit your horizons to a small puddle, surrounded by hot-tempered citizens. "It's like wine," she says, sipping her fifth glass. "There are seas with fishier, saltier, heavier or lighter flavors. I love pasta cooked in our sea."

Also the sound of the waves hitting the beach—I have never heard it like that before. Like two sounds mixed together: a carpet someone is dragging over a bed of pebbles, back and forth, combined with fragments of the frequency produced by plastic bottles being crinkled.

"This is our special place," Clara gets back on the righteous path and spews the required speech. "Half an hour and you are in La Palma, a very impressive place. A biosphere reserve, like many areas here. You can hike to no end. You will get a good deal here."

After the bill and the tip, I ask for a few more minutes to wander among the souvenir shops. I'm not looking for anything specific, just going through everything that's sold in them. Cups, key chains, bottle openers and jewelry, trinkets containing volcanic soil, t-shirts. Clara urges me to get going, as they are waiting for us in the next house.

We head from the boardwalk towards the car. At the center of the trail stands a large group of smiling people wearing floral clothes. Tourists speaking loudly in English gathered around one man. He looks so familiar to me. Very similar to one Andy I used to work with. Andy with the Dalí mustache and eternal charisma. I want to know if it's him.

"We don't have time, you know." Clara pulls me away almost by force and drags me into the car. We turn on the ignition. "Sorry if I was rude, OK? You're right. Sometimes it's very tiring to grow up in a place where you don't always have room to escape from all these tourists. So you have to know when to cut them off and when to get what you need out of them. One learns."

"Don't you sometimes want to get out of here? You said you do a little traveling."

"Sir, I know my profession very well. I am the best. I know this whole island by heart. Why would I want to get out of here? We are driving up the road towards Vilaflor, which is 1,400 meters above sea level. I think you will really like this house," she says confidently.

We enter an intersection by a small gas station that has a souvenir and convenience store at the front, with a few tourists inside. The view is truly impressive and breathtaking. Then we continue to climb the road a little more. The small houses in the villages are painted in different colors and meander through the streets together with us. They dwindle little by little.

Clara tells me to stop at some distance from the houses. We park with the front of the car higher than the back. The leg muscles struggle to walk up slightly above the turn. The entrance to the house is isolated, slightly hidden and enclosed between two other houses, but not adjacent to them. I feel a little disappointed, like we are repeating the same pattern.

As soon as Clara turns the bolt and opens the door, something changes. We enter a small corridor that curves several feet. Then a completely different house reveals itself ahead. "This is the back entrance," Clara explains. "If you become the owner of the house, you can use a different one."

The house stands on a cliff, a two-story tower. Of wide dimensions. The surface of the wall facing the opening from which we entered is pockmarked with depressions and bumps, valleys and hills from the carved rock that formed the short tunnel we walked through. The walls are a soft, fresh light green color. They are combined with wooden windows clasping the frosted glass allowing a pleasant light to flow in. The living room exits to the balcony.

Clara asks me to go up to the second floor first. I go up wooden stairs painted in the same color. Upstairs I find the bathroom, bedrooms painted orange-yellow with wardrobes and small wooden chests in the colors of the windows. We go back down.

"I wanted you to see. This house is isolated. It is special. Go out on the balcony and feel it." Clara reads me like an open book. I go outside. I inhale a lungful of air and glance back. The front and sides are covered in ivy. Beyond the fences are the neighbors' gardens, but they all seem to be a bit farther apart. The house stands nobly elevated above its peers, overlooking the amazing view from the height of the village.

"Wait. This isn't all," she says, speaking like a seasoned TV host. The previous houses were the build-up to sweep me away in awe now. She wanders with me through a kitchen painted in warm colors, and with windows that light up the eyes. "The price is one hundred and fifty thousand euros, and we can talk to the owner about a discount if you pay cash. But I wanted to show you something important."

She points to what is under the balcony. Rows of vines hanging on wires. "These are wine grapes," she throws in the punch line. "There are people who tend to them. You get the whole package: the house, the land and the small winery. You don't have to worry about anything. There is a tenant who takes care of everything, sells it, and transfers your part to you. It's a tiny winery that sells a small number of bottles each year."

The sophisticated Clara, an experienced professional, hit me with a hammer and charmed me with a stunning house and a balcony whose view one can only dream of.

A place that seems quiet and a bit isolated, yet is not very far from the cities and towns below. An affordable price and even the chance to make an income on the side. I ask her for a moment to myself. She goes up to the second floor and leaves me with the view and the air inside my lungs. I'm trying to imagine it. Trying to stop the tide in my heart, the feeling that here, it may be happening.

I pull out my happiness notebook, in which I have so far written two words. A word on each page: TRANQUILITY and LANDSCAPE, and add the word ELEVATION. I call Clara. "Thank you. It really is a special place and I might go for it. Can I meet the owner?" Clara makes a few calls and informs me that she has arranged a meeting with the seller at a local restaurant in the evening.

A few hours later, all showered, optimistic and smelling good, I arrive at the Casa Peña restaurant. The owner invites me. "Take whatever you want," she says. Even though it's cold, we're sitting on the patio. The atmosphere convinces me to stay outside. We have a pleasant conversation about the house and the village. I'm enchanted by her personality. She jokes with me in proper English and gossips about the neighbors. Then she says that she divorced her husband a long time ago.

"I also have experience with strangers," she laughs. "My son is in Playa de las Américas. He sails a small boat for tourists who want to watch the dolphins. His partner is Greek. She's a tour guide and also manages the cruises."

She asks me about my background. I tell her a little about my professional past, the advertising agency and my country. I tell her about a corrupt politician I once worked with and she tells me about the mayor of one of the islands who really stinks. We compare beaches, and very quickly slide into annoying things people do in a queue or in a restaurant. She shares with me adventures from her son's resort area, which remind me a little of Blue Beach.

I feel that the time is right and she seems willing. I raise the issue of the house and ask for a small reduction in the asking price. I explain to her the complexity and the move I need to make here. I still don't know what it all entails, and I'll have to figure out how to arrange for the purchase and what taxes to pay. "But I like it," I add and ask: "Try to do your best." She promises to think about it.

The evening is getting colder, the last diners are already finishing. "Can you tell me a little about the vineyard and the winery?" I ask. She asks for the bill and suggests that we do it at the house itself.

We are standing on the terrace holding a glass of Chardonnay from her winery. Small distant lights decorate the evening. Far, far away I see the lights of boats. I feel optimistic. Maybe because the happiness diary is starting to work. Maybe because of the peace in this place. Maybe because of the balcony overlooking such a beautiful, lush landscape. Maybe it's the isolated house working its magic on me.

"Why exactly are you here?" She starts the conversation by shooting an accurate arrow right on the target. "Why did you come all the way from your country to buy a house here? I hope it's okay that I ask." I decide not to hide anything. To say something simple and true. "I'm looking for peace. A year ago my son, Lake, died of a brain tumor. He was such a sensitive child, he smiled so much and was also so curious. Much of what was in his heart went through his intellect. Quite often this was his way of expressing love."

"You don't remember your child in formulas," she determined.

"No. I remember every minute of cuddling. Every hug. Every sob when he was injured. I remember how he glided down the ziplines without any fear. In general, it seemed there were many things he did not fear. I also remember the silence and modesty that sometimes hid an inner turmoil. I'm just getting carried away, a bit too much." I stop myself for a moment, then add: "I'm considering moving here."

She looks at me with a deep gaze. Not a romantic look, but rather one that shows understanding. As if despite having known each other for two hours only, there is a tacit alliance between us, a connection.

"You didn't get carried away at all, you could have done worse," her eyes grow wider. Her gaze is captivating. She does not move her body or her face, just looks straight at me. "I founded the winery four years ago. At first it was just me, with the help of a few employees. I worked in pruning, tilling, and watering. I also failed quite a bit. It began as occupational therapy."

"Can I ask what you were healing from?" I return her gaze with a request with a form duly filled out and signed by a notary to certify honesty and authenticity.

"I've been struggling with mental illness," she says without bowing her head or being embarrassed, in a way that surprises me. "On the whole, my life was going well, but the difficult moments of the outbreaks of my condition happened unexpectedly. My ex-husband and I purchased this place to give me peace of mind. Like the peace you're looking for maybe. He bought himself another place and divorced me. My son lives elsewhere and I stayed here. Then I read about the Kilauea plan."

"The Kilauea plan?"

"In 2018, the Kilauea volcano erupted in Hawaii. We live here right next to Teide, our local volcano. I was curious to learn about it. It all started with earthquakes that created fissures around the volcano, even dozens of miles away. A volcano has a magma chamber, an underground reservoir of molten rock which rises and falls according to its activity. After the eruption, the level in this chamber dropped, reached the groundwater and caused the collapse of enormous rock walls. Imagine that even these rocks could no longer withstand the pressure coming from below, so that the huge eruption created could be seen on satellite photos, from ships and from planes flying very far from Hawaii.

"Following the eruption, the US launched the Kilauea program in which 161 active volcanoes in the country are constantly monitored. An amazing program that uses sensors, helicopters, navigation software, seismographs and many other technologies and tools. It fascinated me. I read about it over and over. You could say people thought I was crazy. They didn't understand why I was so obsessed with it."

I giggle. "As you know, only Jews can tell Jewish jokes, only twenty-one-year-old patients with a brain tumor can say that they entered the disease incredibly healthy, and only mentally challenged people can say that they think they are crazy."

"That's when I realized I needed my Kilauea plan. A program that, if implemented, could help me manage my outbursts. So I asked everyone I could what the early signs of my outbreaks were, so I could predict them or maybe avoid them. I found out what keeps me balanced and calms me down."

There are people whose mere presence in a room changes something in the atmosphere. And she is one of them. She radiates inexplicable energy. Speaks with passion. I am fascinated by her original idea. I sense the house is like that too. It runs some mysterious energy, some quiet charisma within its walls.

"I won't torture you by talking about the preliminary signs and the sensors I put on myself. That's a story in itself," she continues and I take in her words eagerly. "But I will say that I also asked them what constrains, calms and keeps me balanced. I was told all kinds of little things until, one day, I arrived at my older sister's house and she told me something I didn't remember at all. She said how at the age of three, four or five I would disappear for hours. They found me sitting in the heart of my family's vineyard, basking in the dirt, caressing the plants, playing with insects, sitting in puddles, picking grapes. I found myself sitting in my bed at night and replaying these moments, and realized that this was it. I went from the madness of Kilauea to the madness of grapevines."

"Wow, that's amazing!" I say, not hiding my admiration. I drain the rest of the wine from the glass in my hand and fill it a little more from the bottle resting on the balcony railing.

"I prune, nurture, read about pests, study the different varieties. I go down to the little vineyard I have here facing the balcony and do my occupational therapy. That's how I got to wine. Pruning, sorting, processing, aging in barrels and bottling. A good friend told me that sometimes pregnancy balances mentally challenged woman. Since I started to work at the vineyard and the winery, it seems like I'm in an eternal pregnancy. Like embryos develop in the belly of the garden and then are born into barrels and, from there, into bottles until we ship them." She pronounces the last sentences with a smile, raises her glass at an angle and sips more of the wine. She even strokes her belly over her dress for a moment.

This may seem like a romantic scene. Wine. A sense of connection. A view that has an effect on the body. But my romance originates from the feeling that this house could be mine. Maybe I found my real estate partner. I stay silent, sipping a little more wine. She is silent too.

"How about spending the night in the apartment here?" she offers after a few minutes of speechless sipping. "You, ok? Not us," she hurries to correct a proposal that could be interpreted differently.

"Fantastic idea!" I reply with enthusiasm. We go to the bedroom. She arranges pillows, blankets and sheets for me. She turns on the heating. We go down to the entrance floor. She places the key in the door from the inside, writes me the name of the store where I can buy some groceries, and asks me to call in the morning after I've explored the surroundings a bit.

"You said at dinner that you were fit," she says just before closing the door behind her. "So I recommend you climb the Sombrero. It's about fifteen minutes from here. Higher up. You will see a unique view. Call me when you reach the top of the Sombrero, tell me what you feel."

Chapter 15

Almost two weeks in Tenerife. Fresh from a deep sleep induced by the house wine, I get up in the morning and go to the Sombrero. It's a challenge for my legs. Slope by slope of broken stones. I climb and await the moment the house owner promised me.

"I'm on the top of the Sombrero," I finally say to her, waiting for a response from the other end of the line.

"Wonderful. Turn your head around and look at 360 degrees of this amazing diversity. Have you seen the sea from my house? Behind the Sombrero there are pine trees and rare bushes. And what's on the other side?"

I'm really amazed. The Teide reveals itself in full glory. Between us extends a wide desert orange-brown crater. I am filled with the feeling of the immense, tireless force of nature. "It's truly beautiful," I say.

The wind occasionally distorts the communication. In the meantime, I pull out my happiness notebook and write the fourth word in big letters, on the fourth page. DESERT. What a magnificent desert landscape.

"So tell me, why are you selling the house, actually? It calms you down, doesn't it?"

"I will be completely honest with you, as I have until now." She does not hesitate this time either. "Recently, several branches were axed off and the vineyard suffered some damages. I thought it was animals, because sometimes there is howling at night. Until I caught a group of youngsters doing it and realized what was going on. And this is the least happy part of this whole story. My neighbors didn't particularly like my outbursts. They claim that my behavior has been bringing down the value of their property. I haven't had an attack in a long time, but they have their own views. Our compromise was that I can rent out the vineyard to a tenant and sell the house to someone else, but I have to move out."

I mumble the words to *Heard it Through the Grapevine*.

"What's that?" she asks.

"Never mind," I answer. "I get it. I totally get it. They won't do that to me. I am the solution. Not the problem. I understand." I repeat it to make sure the message is clear, and then end the conversation saying I'll think about the next steps and will be in touch with her.

I enjoy the quiet. The tranquility. The distance. The height. Too bad one can't build a house here. Atop the Sombrero a mother and probably her young daughter, are climbing up. They spread a large, worn blanket on the rocky surface. Lay down some cushions. Take out sandwiches, fruit and drinks. They talk to each other and laugh. I smile. It is beautiful and heartwarming to watch the bond they share.

After a few minutes they invite me to join them and hand me a cushion to sit on. I look at this playground that is all waves of land crashing into the wind. The rocks are scattered like giant Legos across the whole area. Hills of sharp slices, pyramids and cones. Blue, red, orange and yellow, black and white.

I pull out my phone to take a picture, and also to save

the location on the map. When I swipe away the missed calls, I recognize a phone number that I don't see often. God's personal assistant. She calls occasionally, but not often. Most of the time God himself sends me a message when he needs me, or I call him and we talk. This is reserved for rare cases. She called five times.

To be on the safe side, I return to my WhatsApp messages. There is one from her saying God tried to reach me several times and asked her to set up a call for us. This is important, she stresses, and adds the appropriate emoji. In the background I hear the mother giving her daughter math problems to solve. She hugs her and says "well done" when the young woman gets them right. She's tutoring her or showing her how to get to the solution. One doesn't have to know the language to understand that the dialogue goes somewhere along those lines. My stomach is churning.

Then she calls again. My eyes are getting misty. The phone's buzzing doesn't go away. God's assistant is calling me here. I'm on the Sombrero and she insists. Because when someone acquires you, they own you wherever you may be. I have been running around for five days looking for a home, and home catches up with me everywhere I go. I asked questions about the cost of living and recycling. I was looking for panoramic views. For people. I applied myself to the tasks again. To the objectives. To clarifying the details. To reducing the dimensions of uncertainty. And the typhoon gets stronger again. It comes looking for you. There is a knock on your door. They want something from you. And it knocks on your door too—like it or not.

I'm sitting on the edge of the Sombrero and my eyes are watering. Everything collapses like a house of cards. I have no energy for God now and I have no energy to deal with the pain that overwhelms me. This faucet is like a spring that never runs dry. A perpetuum mobile[3] of pain and tears that won't let go of me.

I try to ignore it. I smile at the mother and daughter. But my heart stabs me again. How can one not get goosebumps from seeing a young blonde girl with blue eyes solving calculus problems? The mighty Teide volcano rises before me in the distance. A huge, sandy plain and impressive valley separates us. Acres of aridity that can change at any moment. After more than a week on this island I am again chasing my own tail in circles and can't crack the puzzle. And the worst thing is that I hide it from myself. I'm all sombrero and no cattle.

A man with a successful career, who has already solved incredibly complex puzzles, who has written the sharpest messages for others and told the right stories—fails to solve his own puzzle. Standing frustrated on the tip of a thorn. Wherever I turn, the voice of my son's blood crieth unto me from the ground. If only I could try and rewrite this story. Get up without the pain.

I wonder when I will exhaust myself enough to get up early in the morning with a new song in my heart.

The greatest riddle solver was Lake. One day, a little before he turned three, I took him with me to the office. An impressive villa, a safe space covered in wall-to-wall carpeting, fancy bookcases and heavy wooden doors. Lake ran around pleased with himself, returning to me every now and then to say hello. At noon he suddenly disappeared. I looked for him until I heard a sound from

---

3   A perpetually moving machine

the bathroom. It turned out that he had locked the door from the inside and couldn't open it. For twenty minutes we looked for solutions, gave him suggestions, until finally I called the janitor. Just seconds before we broke the door down, Lake strolled out completely at ease, with his golden smile, and modestly said that he had managed to release the jammed lock.

At the age of nine, he excitedly ran from statue to statue in Rome, and explained to us the story of each one. Its name in Greek mythology and how it was called in Roman mythology. When he was ten years old, long before WAZE and even Google, he navigated around London, which we were visiting for the first time in his life, using paper maps. To the wax museum and then back to the hotel, while I lay in bed with a fever.

Lake is the one who played chess, taught himself origami and programming languages, cracked complex sudoku games, assembled Rubik's cube and solved riddles and logic puzzles on Saturday mornings. Lake found YouTubers who invited viewers to games where they had to crack complex puzzles or guess by following clues. I've never seen anyone talk so excitedly about the Bernoulli or Poisson distribution.

The daughter rests her head on her mother's shoulder, and the two watch the space spread out in front of them. The mother explains something to her, pointing in different directions. The daughter listens, taking in the view, absorbing the information.

I take my earphones out of the bag. I turn on the music and wait as always for it to help me. To be my friend and brother. To build a path for me and be a shoulder I can lean on. When Sharon Lifshitz sings about Tot, it reminds me that as much as he was moved by the Poisson distribution, he was moved by fantasies, creatures and imaginary wars. Lake was also excited by gatherings and conventions where he met people who are as excited as he was by the same things. It was the people-loving Lake, who traveled by train with a sword or cloak and spent nights in a sleeping bag up north.

I was reminded of a song that struck me when I heard it at an international song festival once, and I looked up the meaning of its lyrics, written by one Dan Toren:

> *A cold silence faces the solar wind,*
> *Eyes veiled in mist,*
> *Voices of a lost battle rise from yesterday's field,*
> *Tut gazes at the red-hued light.*

I set my hydration pack down on a rock and put my head on it. Slowly. Cautiously.

> *A king plays a part, an actor's role,*
> *Not born to live alone,*
> *A solo show for many actors,*
> *Who've never learned not to expect a throne.*

> *Three black dogs guard from the bridge's north,*
> *Tut descends in the evening to the sea,*
> *On the mountain, the eagle and vulture cross,*
> *Eyes fill with blood, a grim decree.*

I close my eyes for a moment. Letting the wind caress my face. At varying speeds, in changing directions. Letting the ears hear the friction with its movement. And the hair on the head rising and falling at changing rates.

> *Tut will go this evening, as always, to the castle,*
> *To hear a call—"Your son is dead."*
> *With a silver sword, he steps onto the stage,*
> *To face it alone, as he has said.*
> *A cold bow before the applauding crowd,*
> *Eyes veiled in mist,*
> *Voices of a lost battle fade from the lips,*
> *Tut now weeps, witnessed by none.*[4]

The young woman lightly touches my shoulder, drawing my attention with infinite gentleness. "I'm so sorry," she says. They must leave.

I get up. The prisms in the field change their light and shimmer in the setting sun. I walk down the mountain carefully. Trying to find a place to spend the charge accumulated in my daily battery. The one that brings me back again and again to the erupting volcano. The one that manages my happy calendar which syncs with another one, an unbearably difficult one.

* * *

I had promised Clara I would give her an answer about the house. I call her. "This house is a viable option I am considering, but let's continue."

Here. I had written all the words that made me a little happy. I put them all together in a perfect house, but

---

[4] *"Tot" Lyrics by Dan Toren*

it all collapsed like a house of cards from Lake's magic trick kits.

"Listen, Mister," Clara says when we meet again, losing some of her European politeness likely due to the feeling that she might have lost a potential commission. "I've invested quite a bit of time in you. You have to make your mind up and choose."

I stammer, taken aback because I hadn't thought of this possibility. She raises her hand, places one of her fingers by my throat and presses in a way that hurts me. "I didn't waste days on you to come out with nothing." Her face comes closer to mine. A face that previously dripped honey in every interaction we had. The face of a real estate expert who is focused on sales and knows how to bridge between people. The face became rigid. Frozen cheeks. Pursed lips. Narrowing eyes. The brim of the hat bends in front of my forehead. She's shorter than me, but that doesn't make her less intimidating.

"I'll give you one more suggestion. Drive to Masca. See the place. If you feel it's for you, I'll find you a home there. It's a small area. It will be more complicated, but it's a very special place. You should go there. And you'll pay me extra in commissions. Double." She loses her patience and makes it clear she won't be joining me.

"Yes, yes. Absolutely," I hasten to agree, trying to end this meeting as quickly as possible.

At sunset I drive on the road back north. The sea is on my right. Hunger is gnawing at me. I haven't eaten all day. I climbed the Sombrero. I let the car drive at a moderate speed, arrive at Santa de la Cruz and wander the streets for an hour or so. In such cases there is only one solution, I tell myself. Pizza. A bubbling Teide of boiling, cheesy, tomatoey, volcanic activity. With hard basaltic edges that sting the tongue. From time to time, splashes of beer will be squirted into my mouth at nearly freezing temperatures like on the peak of the Teide.

I can't say very much about that evening. I can only recommend, if you are ever in Tenerife, that you go to Mamma Mia's in the La Laguna neighborhood. For the first time in my life, I devoured an entire tray of pizza all by myself.

Chapter 16

That afternoon, at the end of Tenerife's only southbound highway, I turn from the Santiago del Teide road towards a village called Masca, which sits at the gateway of Los Gigantes. Goats cross the road during all hours of the day, forcing me to concentrate. At every turn one must look carefully, predicting the future, anticipating the slightest gestures that may precede a crash. Three and a half miles. My car shrinks a little whenever another vehicle approaches from the opposite direction, holding itself taut and precise. Every inch counts.

When I roll into the parking lot, the sun is about to set. In the past, Masca was a Guanche village. The ancient settlers of the island who lived there cultivated small plots of land along the mountainsides. It is assumed they came from Africa. In the sixteenth century, pirates captured the area. From the village, the rocks of Los Gigantes open up, like an inverted triangle revealing the sea that is almost eight hundred meters below it. The pirates would go down the paths to the rare beach with the small stones and black sand, to emerge with their ships from among the rocks into the sea and ambush ships sailing near the Canary Islands. They would then return with the booty and carry it up the road along the steep slope, to the village.

Even in the twentieth century the village could only be reached by walking for about four miles, either up from the beach or between the mountains. Only in the 1970s was a dirt road built along this route, which became an actual road in the 1980s.

The parking lot is teeming with buses and tourists ready to watch the imminent sunset. I go into a small restaurant called *Encontré Mi Lugar*, right on the road, to find out where my B&B is. A local couple gives me some directions. "But wait," says the tall, bespectacled bearded man, who gives the impression of being the owner of the place. "Don't rush. Treat yourself to a beer. Watch the sunset. It'll bring out everything you have inside. It's something special."

I know this speech is intended for tourists, but I don't care. I nod. He pulls down the beer handle and pours. I turn my eyes towards the horizon and head close to the edge of the road. Among the giggling tourists are a romantic couple kissing, and several children. Lucky that here it's legitimate to be sad. It isn't anywhere else. For the few days following the funeral, it's perfectly fine. Even a week or a month later. Then they tell you—you have a family, a job, great hobbies, you have something to live for. Life is so beautiful. Come, I'll take you to a good show, to a movie. Let's go dancing. They pat you on the back in an understanding manner. Let's be merry. They throw in a good joke.

Sometimes you also respond with cynicism or humor. The bereaved are allowed to joke about death. To act like a clown who tackles everything with humor is perfectly fine. Everyone loves at least one buffoon at work or among their friends. The one who drops the joke right on the spot even if everyone is horribly embarrassed. There is also the one who's always complaining. Or the one who is quiet most of the time, until she throws in a super smart quip that makes you think there is a limited quota of words in the world, and she uses hers very well.

So, funny sells big time. But sad? It is neither convenient nor productive. And no one feels like consoling anyone. How much can you console? How original can you be when doing so? I feel sorry for your loss. OK, we said it. And now what? And it's not that bad if it's your mom, dad or grandparent. They are supposed to go at some point. But your son or daughter?!

No. He did not die in war or in battle. He has no memorial, except for a few chemo pills forgotten in a drawer. He wasn't in any high-risk group. Just a falling star. There is no story of heroism. Why do they even say that someone who is ill is a hero? Where is the heroism in that? "Gentlemen," says the officiant at the ceremony, "he could have chosen not to be sick and go watch some NBA games instead, but he was relentless and decided to be ill. To go for the fight."

Holding the glass in my hand I look at the inverted triangle that captures the sun sliding down its cyclical path, like it does every day, towards the sea. I use the glass as the mediator through which my gaze passes. The glass changes its angle, the beer touches my lips. They meet the brown liquid, like the beach meets the waves. The resulting prism mediates the sun to me. Some of it is swallowed by the murky brownness of the beer, darkening it. Some of its rays bend when passing through the thick glass and distort it. And in the upper part, it leaves me blinded by the glitter.

This is the way it goes now. Half of your body is immersed in the bitterness of the wall that entraps you time and time again, while the other half tries with all its might to retake life, as if nothing stood in the way of the blinding sun. But some huge weight hanging over your body simply won't let go.

The sun dips into the sea, wades for a bit, and then dives in. Maybe here, I say to myself, maybe here I will get some rest. I will become resident number one hundred and ninety-nine of the village. Every evening I will watch the sunset with a beer to quench my thirst for incessant crying. For the perpetuum mobile of tears, sorrow, grief, pain. I will drink gallons of tranquility while lazily watching visiting tourists bask in the sun and disappear on cloudy days, leaving us to ourselves.

Chapter 17

The silence wakes me up. It's got a no-one scattered across my temporary home, between the white walls and the red-brown tiles. A little before sunrise, which happens here around half past seven, I'm ready. I'm cushioned by my running shoes. Ventilated by my pants and shirt.

Intent on my mission, I drive off. The second time on the three-and-a-half-mile twists and turns that separate Masca from Santiago del Teide feels different. The up and downhill segments iron themselves out before me. I'm already used to the brotherhood of drivers who make way for one other ahead of time. Each winding ascent turns out to be a thread connecting between the two mountain villages, and is vital for their social development. Codes of behavior, a common denominator. Heritage. You already say to yourself, this is the viewpoint half way there. Is the fruit vendor going to be there today, as usual?

At the end of the descent, once in Santiago del Teide, the city is lively and warm. I roll down the window. It's Friday. The aromas of cooking rise from the city streets. My grandmother might have said that they were preparing a meal for an extended family gathering. I have a friend, a meat lover without frontiers, who would add: "Jam-packed with jamón."[5]

---
5   Ham in Spanish

I park the car on a side street in the outskirts of the town by a chain of narrow white houses with small courtyards and black doors. There are only three or four cars. While I'm getting my things, a man who looks about a decade older than me emerges from one of the houses. He waves goodbye to someone at home, and greets me with an "Hola" in a heavy British accent. His running clothes are a little sloppy, a small belly peeking out through them. He puts on sunglasses and immediately covers his shining baldness with a hat.

I answer my "Hola" politely and put on my earbuds. Trying to become absorbed into my world, with myself. I let the music flow as I run between the low stone fences on the path overlooking the distant mountains. Behind me, the Brit starts running too.

At first I jog, skipping the small stones, using them as a basalt trampoline. The gap between me and the Brit widens. He moves a little farther away from me. The town is at an altitude of about 3,000 feet. The Chinyero volcano is almost 1,800 feet higher. Soon this picnic run will end and the route will change.

After about two thirds of a mile, the steeper slopes begin. But I don't slow down or relax. The easy run is now combined with strenuous walking. Side by side, the pace of the trail and my breathing cycle beat in unison. Competing with or complementing each other, who knows. Each leg moving from a height of eight inches to the ground shakes the body for a moment, forcing the muscles to inhale a pump-full of oxygen. Every landing makes a muffled sound. Every unlevel step or narrow creek needs the impetus of swinging arms.

The temperature outside is only sixty-eight degrees,

but the sun of the Canary Islands is bright, burning, open, without filters. It dazzles me. My inner self aims for the top. Don't ask me to teach you, because I wouldn't know how to. My body learned this over twenty five years of running. I'm there until the rubber of my sneakers does us part.

My legs skip alternatingly. My hamstrings scream in protest, but I ignore them. The gluteus burns out. My buttocks are on fire. Every second it feels like I'm stumbling. In my mind, a disaster is about to happen. I'm going to trip, my legs will slip, and my body will fall flat on the stones. But it doesn't happen.

The balance of horror between me and the sharpening hard spongy sole is getting stronger. I threaten to injure them, and they threaten to injure me. The water burbles inside my hydration pack. My breath explodes. There is no room in my body for all the oxygen I need right now. The music in my ears screams progressive, psychedelia, rock. Everything erupts, angry and stormy. This time I won't show the body any consideration, I decide. This time I will be considerate of myself. This time I won't hold back. This time, everything that's inside will come out.

My muscles are like a regular contestant on Survivor. Everyone is a partner in the effort. Everyone, including everyone. Even the tiny stapedius, a muscle that's only a few millimeters long, located in the middle ear.

The ground finally becomes level for a moment. The crossroads instructs me to continue uphill. I turn right and look ahead to the road. Then, little by little, it reveals itself to me. After about four miles my feet step into the killing field. My consciousness perceives that I am not standing here alone. Standing with me are millions of witnesses to what has taken place hundreds of times. At the very least, certainly from the eighth century AD until recently. A huge black park.

I run across the terrain. My legs are like shock-absorbing springs, pushing ahead. Ibrahim Maalouf is trumpeting *Beirut* in my ears. Among the smoky embers on the trails, my mind floats back to times past. It's the holiday season. Lake is next to me in the narrow, yellow room. The doctor appears on the screen in front of us. Lake tells him about the medication that's having no effect. His questions are innocent. Brief. Humbly accepting his fate. His speech is encumbered, nullified by mouth muscles that no longer function. I take on the role of interpreter. The doctor replies in short, quiet sentences.

The road is black. The soles of my light-colored shoes dig into the pointed, charred basalt crumbs that hurt my feet and collide with my ankles.

Lake doesn't cry. He just nods in understanding. The image on the computer monitor goes off. We exchange a few short words. "Dad," he finally says, "if so, I won't take the medicine today." He screams the words in absolute silence, until my ears burst. While he is sitting up I hold him in a hug. His bent-down profile softens towards me for a moment. If only I could shatter into thousands of pieces right now, and scatter among these fragments of powerful 100%-dark chocolate without a single drop of sweetness. If only it were possible to sit here on one of the rocks. Every rock here stings, sharp, stabbing. A fucking *fakir* paradise. Let everything stab and scream. I still wouldn't be able to experience even a fraction of the pain of that conversation anyway.

Exhausted, I stop for a moment to catch my breath

and, while I'm looking for a place in the shade, I see him approaching me with measured steps. I hasten to wipe away the tips of tears welled up in my eyes.

The Brit pushes the sunglasses sliding from sweat and sunscreen closer to his eyes. As part of an unexplained alliance between runners who keep each other company, he stops too. It's a good time to drink a little and have something to eat. I pull the earbuds out of my ears and take out the snack bag I prepared. Dried fruits, peanuts and walnuts.

"Fancy a drink?" he asks with a toothy smile, handing me a tube. "A sip of whiskey, bloke." I politely refuse.

"Fuck. I don't feel like running. Steak and chips, that's what I fancy." He can barely catch his breath. And then smiles. I smile back.

"What... do you see?" he asks like the start of a Monty Python sketch. With a pause after the declarative 'what' and then the words that end up an octave higher.

No polite questions like what's your name or where are you from. "Lava? Volcanic rock?" I answer with hesitation.

"And what don't you see?" he continues in the same tone of voice. I'm trying to figure out where he's going with this. I look around for a minute. Outside my headphones, the wind and silence are present in full force. The sea in the distance, the village below.

And then I get it. "There are no plants here," I mumble to myself, then repeat my realization aloud: "No flowers."

"Good answer, chap," he gently pats my back, signaling that he is very pleased with my answer. "The last eruption took place in November 1909. A ten-day eruption. It is well documented. There are pictures of people riding donkeys and collecting burning coals produced from the trees on the edge of the lava to heat their homes. Just imagine this. On the one hand, a stream that devastates and kills every living thing. And on the other hand, people who live on its fringes. It's an unimaginable dissonance."

"Are you a risk-taker or something?" I wonder. He replies with a smile. I state my name and add where I'm from and tell him that I recently did some work in Congo.

"Josh. Geologist. I'm a volcanologist, mate. If you were in Congo, then you're the risk-taker, aren't you? The missus and I have been in the Canaries for ten years, going from place to place. It's heaven for us." He says the last words in a half-whisper, closing his eyes a little, to stress his point.

"But, like you said, the volcano has not been active for a hundred years." I immediately harness my curiosity to steal new information.

"I've seen advertisements: 'Come to Congo. Geology. Wildlife. Gorillas. Okapi. Bonobos.'" Not five minutes have elapsed and already my new friend, the British geologist, has something to say about my geographical choices. "Are you sure this is the case? Don't they have a conflict there? I heard that there are terror attacks almost every day."

"Listen, Josh. It's much more complex than that. Personal security is at a very high level and... " I start a sentence but actually I really don't feel like talking about politics right now. I prefer to stay on volcanoes.

"No worries mate. I wasn't going to criticize or anything. It's the same here. Only that an active volcano is bad for business. There are five million tourists here every year. So the governor of the Canaries founded a research institute that constantly checks the state of the mountain, and he also yells at UNESCO: 'Why do you say the mountain is active?' Did you know that he unilaterally declared the mountain dormant?"

I would now like to be a geologist of the kind that goes hiking in the mountains, and returns every day to his beloved wife, who awaits with tea or whiskey. If, for a moment I was worried, he makes it clear to me that everything works here 24/7. A year and a half ago the volcano erupted on the neighboring island of La Palma, in 2004 high levels of volcanic particles were recorded in this area and, if I go up to Teide, I will see several points of rising smoke.

"OK. This is very interesting, but just take me back to the plants. Why are there no plants? You yourself said that more than a hundred years have gone by."

"It's only been one century. It takes hundreds. I liked to tell my students that there is life. Soil. Greenery. Plants. Trees," he enjoys playing Shakespearean theater with himself. "Suddenly—a huge event. Quakes. Enormous amounts of energy. Unimaginable temperatures. You know, those shocking events that happen to people once in a lifetime? Boiling lava crawling down the mountain slopes. The Titanic of geology. It comes from the core of the earth. I would like to visit the core of the Earth once. If here it is paradise, there it is the most hellish of hells. Can't be at the core, so at least as close as possible. Everything spurts, erupts and covers only a particle of a sphere. But it's your piece of land that died there, the one piece of land you cultivated for generations."

Josh takes a break for a drink, perhaps to cool his own enthusiasm. Maybe to lower the volume in which he's talking to me. He tightens the bag on his back, and says quietly: "For three hundred years, sometimes heavy rains will fall here and sometimes just a drizzle. Sometimes there will be strong winds here and sometimes flying creatures will come by, tiny animals that carry in their legs or scatter material they brought with them—rot, soil, moss and stubborn seeds that will soak up water that has just been trapped."

You feel that he really likes doing that—delivering a lecture. "It will happen slowly in our terms, but quickly in your terms," I state what I understand.

"And, in the end, there will be land, my lad, fertile soil where you can grow fruits and vegetables, amazing ones. The best soil there is. All this pain will eventually do good things for someone. And to tell the truth, actually, all along the way. Because for that you need all these good things—rain, wind, sunshine, rot, bees, plants, seeds. These are good things."

After the birds and the bees conversation he asks what I do in life.

"I work in strategic consulting. You could call it advertising."

"So you're a doctor too. A spin doctor?" He uses an expression common in Europe about professionals in my line of business. I tactfully ask him if one can make a reasonable living as a geologist.

"It's okay, you don't need to beat around the bush. You must make good money," he laughs bitterly. "I said paradise, but that's on the professional side. My wife works remotely a little, as a data scientist. Not everyone is willing to hire a person who never sets foot in the office. When you're a geology lecturer at a university, the salary is not amazing. Even in the Canaries."

"And your wife? Is she okay with you guys wandering around like this?"

"She married me. I think the hardest part is being far away from the children. I have a son in Boston and one back home in England. We do video calls. But we try to have them come here once every few years. My son says that when the kindergarten teacher asks my grandson where grandpa lives, he says his grandpa lives in Vacations."

He wipes off beads of sweat, then adjusts his hat and glasses. "Only, fuck, a field geologist needs to be in good shape, and I'm constantly at war with my beer belly. The situation in recent years is not the best."

I nod understandingly.

"I am a geologist. I love stones, soil, seisms and bubbles, I love fire. That works great for me regarding food too. In short, anything fried, barbecued, dishes that stay on the stove for a long time. Oh, give me some stew that's been simmering for three days. That thing the Jews of Spain invented, *Hamin*? Give it to me anytime." He pronounces the strong 'H' pretty well for a Brit.

"And you? Are you married?"

"No. Not married." I distance myself from the matter so as not to get in too deep.

"OK. Too bad," he doesn't even ask or assume regarding children. "Pop in some time if you're near the volcano."

We shake hands goodbye. He starts to walk away, and I am left with thoughts about a particle of you that has died and how long it takes for something good to grow from it. I take a few steps farther ahead, put the earbuds back in, and begin to move my legs a little faster into a light jog.

My legs are now carrying themselves to the end point.

One mile. Alanis Morissette plays me her version of the Police's *King of Pain* on Spotify. With every breath, a cold, high wind makes its way from above, flowing through my windpipe and hurting my lungs.

When I look down at the landscape unfolding before me, I tell myself that it's weird. I never knew there were so many shades of black.

Chapter 18

I wake up in the morning without an alarm. I lift the blanket and come out of the warm, soft heat. My casa is cozy. The gusty winds outside hit the square glass borders framed by fragrant wooden sashes. There is a slight tremor in the window panes and a barely audible whistling.

It's dark. I naively think I've woken up too early. But no, on the contrary. It's already half past eight. It is clear from the palms. Their trunk base clings firmly to the ground of the steep slope, like a Jeep with its center of mass. Their crowns ooze in the wind, spinning and dancing, flowing in all directions against gravity. Only the mountainsides remain indifferent. Must be their eight million years of experience, I guess. For a moment it seems to me that the short, well-trimmed, green bristles of grass, half an inch long in nature's hair clippers, are standing on end.

It's like watching a disaster being covered on TV. The rain pours non-stop. Uniform drops spaced apart drift in the direction of the wind. An hour later the weather is still stormy, but the light is getting a little brighter. I think this sign can only mean one thing. It's time to repay debts. I put on warm clothes and walk the 1,200 ft between the hanging houses of the Casa and the parking lot of the Masca visitors center.

The wooden benches of *Encontré Mi Lugar* are standing

outside despite the rain. The place is pretty deserted. A family with two small children and a man with his back to me, leaning forward into the cell phone, eagerly reading the screen. I'm sure they'll be happy to earn some income on a day like this.

"Good morning, how are you?" I greet them.

"Hola señor. How is your casa? Are you enjoying the *tranquilidad*?" replies the tall, bearded man, whose name turns out to be Santiago. He introduces me to the staff. David, in the kitchen, behind the coffee machine, and Lucia, the tribe elder.

"I came to sit here for a while. I don't eat much local food like rabbit stew, but I'll have a glass of beer. Maybe even two. Paid, only paid. You were so kind to me, helping me find the casa. Why shouldn't you get something in return?" I say in a celebrational tone.

Santiago fills me a pint. Although it's cool outside, it's still nice that the beer is at a low temperature. I take a light sip of the local bitterness. Since they are not too busy, I wish to learn more about them. Lucia, it seems, cannot stay in one place, no matter how many visitors they have or don't on that day. I ask her in English how long she has been there, and she answers in Spanish using hand gestures and a little help from Google Translate.

I find out that the name of the restaurant means *I've found my place*. A name that could be a title for a streak of potential hits by sight-melting, corny Latin singers. Lucia has been working here for forty years. Her parents were born here. Their parents also farmed the land on this mountain. A wide piece of wood shaped like the upper part of a surfboard hangs on the wall. It's brown, roughly cut, with cone-shaped green bumps jutting out of the surface. Lucia explains to me that it is a small wooden plow that her parents used in their plots. Each had only one small plot. There's only so much you can do on a mountain slope.

Santiago, from the neighboring village, joined thirty years ago. They sell small jars of honey made from local flowers. The restaurant has some basic souvenirs and a booklet on the history of the place. Only in Spanish. Authentic cookies and pastries. The air is filled with the aroma of *Rosquetes de Huevo*, egg-based donuts topped with various fillings, and *Laguneros* , jam-filled almond cookies made in the La Laguna village.

Santiago explains in Spanish mixed with English that he also surrendered to the world a while ago, and shows me lollipops with a TikTok logo.

I try to imagine a lifetime alone in this place. Lucia says her parents helped her build the house. A white brick building with brown basalt stones. When she was twenty they helped her open the restaurant.

Imagine getting up in the morning and walking one minute to your workplace, located on the side of a cliff overlooking the sea. What people call *another quiet day at the office*. Closing the place on days of wild rain and storms because there are no tourists and there is no point. Instead, heat up the house and sit down to read a book or a newspaper.

Maybe this is, after all, what I'm looking for now? Waking up in the morning to a wet or sun-kissed village. Welcoming tourists who ask: "Excuse me, what is there to see here?" "Where should we go for a walk?" "Where is the restroom?" "He won't stop crying, is there a doctor around?"

Once I sit down in the chair, I see him again and recognize him for certain. It's him. It's Andy.

"So it really was you I saw at Playa de la Américas. How, of all places, do I run into you here?"

"The surprising part is that you are here," he retorts. "I'm here all the time."

"What do you mean all the time?"

"I live here. In Tenerife."

Andy came to me many years ago. He didn't want the office, nor the boss. He wanted me. For several weeks I felt like a maiden whose suitor was asking her father for her hand in marriage. It was not easy for my partner to relent on his golden rule: "I decide who manages each assignment in this office." But Andy insisted and, in his special style, paved the way for an agreement that lasted five years.

"Amazing. What made you decide to live here?"

"There is a lot of sun here, for a major part of the year. Comfortable temperatures. A wonderful sea. I have a small yacht moored at Playa de la Américas."

"So do you manage all the business from here? Do you no longer run the business from back home or from other parts of Europe?"

"Less," he says.

I'm impressed by this change. Andy was always a very nice person, but highly wired and antsy. Couldn't sit still for more than ten minutes. Besides, he had a quality reserved for the rarest of persons. Those who can be the complete opposite of you, yet still make you like them. You know, like those villains who are impossible not to like?

"Are you here on a trip?" he asks.

"You could say so," I reply. My mouth wants to add something else, but I stop at that.

"You picked a very good spot here. I love this place. I'm usually in Masca and Los Gigantes at least once a month. Just to stand and drink beer in front of the view, walk around and hike up here. Los Gigantes nourishes me. Like Mother Earth, I swear. Like in the Neil Young song."

I smile. He's always been a politician. Polite, sometimes speaking as an adman and sometimes as a broker. But, in the past, I would never have heard him make a statement like 'Los Gigantes nourishes me' or using a phrase like 'Mother Earth.'

Andy traded in furs. Not just any fur, only natural ones. I mean, the genuine kind. From animals. He always emphasized that he also bought and sold other animal products used in industries like cosmetics or pharmaceuticals. "Only those allowed by law to be killed and then only with a hunting license," he would repeat every chance he got and add a small crease on both sides of his mouth as if he were sweetening some secret. It always seemed to me that he was playing by the Simon Says rules.

"Pardon me, Andy, but what exactly do you mean when you say it nourishes you?"

He smiles calmly again. At first he doesn't say anything, as if he hadn't heard the question. Only the hill of his bald head glimmers in the light of the lamp, emphasizing the gap between it and the hair on the sides above his ears.

"At first I didn't fully understand either. After I moved here, I was on a honeymoon. I was in love and the days went by pleasantly. Then something happened, never mind what exactly right now, and I entered a period of crisis. I was angry and nasty. I myself could not understand what was going on with me. I came here one day a few years ago by chance. It was after everyone on the island had said to me over and over: 'How do you want to be considered a local if you haven't visited Masca and Los Gigantes yet?'

"So, one day, when I was particularly irritated and didn't want to take it out on my partner, I got into the car and left. I drove for miles, nowhere in particular, just to calm down. Until I remembered everything people said about Masca and Los Gigantes and arrived here. I went up the road, sat on the wooden benches. I observed the tourists who came to watch the views. I went for a hike in the forests of Teno Rural Park. I ended the day here drinking beer while facing the sunset. A few weeks later I felt like doing it again. So I went off again. Got on the road again. This time I was more confident. And again I walked in the woods, and again I ended my day here, watching a strip of sea and the sunset.

"A month later I really craved to come up here. I remember waking up in the early morning when it was still dark. I drove like crazy, scraping the twists and turns, almost touching the stones that keep us from falling off the cliff. I heard cars honking at me from the opposite direction. I almost crashed into a bus. Can you believe it? I traversed the five kilometers that separate Santiago del Teide from Masca, and I have no idea how I arrived alive because I drove so fast and recklessly.

"I continued on the narrow road to the park above for another half hour. This time I turned off the cell phone. I wandered through the forest for hours. I headed towards the black cliffs and slopes, and again I ended the day here at this spot with a beer and a sunset. Then I flew down the curves carelessly, my tires screeching at every turn, startling men and women who just wanted to enjoy the view and the magical place, but ran into a local loco.

"When I returned I pondered what this had been about. I thought perhaps it was the road. Maybe I missed the adventures of the past. I'm an entrepreneur, after all, maybe I should start some new venture here? Maybe this was my way of making up for the lack of new thrills? I thought of all kinds of outlets. Today it seems funny to me. For instance, I went gambling every two to three weeks, or challenged myself in some extreme sport. I failed miserably. Both because I'm not very fit and because I don't get along with all kinds of parachutes and surfboards. I opened them upside down, fell off them. You know me. After one surf like that I almost sued someone because I nearly drowned in the sea. In short, I was in the wrong, but we won't tell him that.

"After two months I realized that wasn't it. That just was not the issue. My frustration got so bad that my partner gave up and broke up with me. Then one day I had an idea. I decided to do something different. I went to the beach of Los Gigantes. It's a bay down here. A highly touristic area. Lots of hotels, restaurants. There is a tiny port there, a dock with a lighthouse. I asked one of the boat owner to take me to see the Gigantes from the sea. We left in a small motorboat. After a while it stopped about 300 feet from the cliffs. This huge blackness looked at me from its imposing height. The waves were calm, as they are here most of the time, waves that remind me of a rocking cradle. It's an unbelievable sight. I lifted my head up at an almost impossible angle. The waves padded the black stones very close to the cliff."

Andy narrows his eyes a little. "It's an unbelievable sight," he repeats the words slowly. "I swallowed this sight whole. I drank it and ate it up at the same time. I inhaled it. I asked the boatman to get a little closer. And then a little more. Closer each time. I sat down so as not to fall overboard, closed my eyes for a bit, and opened them again."

Through the open door of the restaurant I see the pouring rain. Andy is deep in the feeling.

"So is this a kind of humbleness? Being in awe of something bigger than you?" I try to decipher his words.

"A feeling of acceptance. Relief..." he said, searching for the exact words. "But wait, it's not just that. It's much bigger than that. I felt it the most when we were really close, and the fisherman was already worried his boat might hit the rocks. I wasn't afraid. I was excited. In the worst case, I thought, my life ends here. Still, we remained there for hours. I pitied the fisherman whom I had asked for a favor, even though I did pay him handsomely so we would head back only at dusk. I stared for hours. Wearing a life jacket, and watching. So yes, there is acceptance and relief, but the closest word I know is originality. An unreplicated copy." His eyes were now only open a slit. His hand rose and pointed to the horizon.

When you search so hard, you want so badly to believe you've found an answer. You cling to every idea, and certainly to an idea formulated so beautifully. There's nothing like a salesman who believes in his product, and Andy was an excellent salesman. He really believed in his product.

Andy came to see me about his idea of establishing an international bingo chain. For this purpose, he first created facts on the ground by opening several small bingo halls in our county. He waited patiently for the police to arrive with a closure order, then hired one of the most prominent lawyers in the country to submit an application to the Supreme Court under the Gambling Prohibition Law. His claim was that there was no gambling going on. Just an entertaining game everyone can enjoy, like the seniors in Seinfeld's Del Boca Vista in Florida.

I'm trying my best to take a deep dive into Andy's idea. All that appears before me, unstoppable and uncontrolled, is the inimitable image of Lake. A one-off character that belongs only to him. I don't say it's good or bad, just his. The times he pronounced a letter that was not exactly in the alphabet, between an R and a W. Not exactly *Run* but not exactly *Won* either. Or when he used to repeat *Can we...?* Can we...? With a perpetual question mark, leaving it hanging in the air. Or *I promised me...* even when he meant to say that someone else had promised him. I, for example.

I barely manage to get up from the table and excuse myself for a moment. Only with difficulty do I escape and go out into the pouring rain, allowing it to beat on my head, without a hat or coat, so that the water mingles with my tears, sorrow, pain, cold, and the constant restlessness that's crumbling once again.

At one point I feel Andy's hand touching my shoulder. "You'll catch a cold, man. Santiago, get the guy a blanket and a heater to warm and dry him up. And he also needs draft beer." As usual, Andy fills the role of the production manager of everything.

"Andy," I say. "I lost my son a year ago."

"Lost him? Do you mean, he died? He passed away?"

"Yes, from a brain tumor." Whenever you say it like

that, in an intellectual tone, it covers the tears well. It takes on a logical form, the kind we like.

"I'm truly sorry." Many really mean it when they say this, but they can't truly be sorry the way they'd like to be sorry. Andy is close enough. "I'm really, really sorry. So sorry."

"I'm here because I had to run away. I had to stop life from going on. I don't know where to store all this pain, all this sorrow, Andy. I'm probably looking for my Gigantes as well. I too was on the top of the world and fell from heaven, and all those worn-out words." A burst of honesty gushed out of me. Sometimes a random person is the right one to tell everything. Even a stranger. Or a reformed criminal. That's also an option.

"I'm really trying to relate to what you said but, Andy, what originality? Is there any originality in the world? Take Arona, for instance. Do you know SEAT's Arona? And all these brand names Americans are so proud of and say they are 'original' names. Nevada, Colorado—what's original about them? What is original about fries and hamburgers, frankfurters and pizza? I've been traveling here for a week and I can't stop laughing."

"Laughing?"

"Laughing, Andy. A Spaniard was traveling around Tenerife, and everything reminded him of something, so he called the towns, bays and mountains like his home. Seriously? It's the start of a joke."

Andy is unfazed by my argument. "I don't believe you really think like that," he says intently. "I don't think you fall into the trap you yourself have set for others for so many years." He adds that he might not have told anyone else what he told me. But I can certainly understand it.

I wipe my face a little. The addictive heat of the small

stove begins to take effect. "I will tell you about a common trap. Well-known. In advertising, it's called recall. You remember something. Like *Coke is It*, for example. Or *We Try Harder*. Avis, right? A proven, much used trick that creates recall. You go for a classic. Once, I was hired by a new phone company. I suggested they launch their first offering before Christmas. Name the brand *Say*, and buy the rights to Stevie Wonder's song. *I just called to say I love you*. The world uses this gimmick all the time."

He still doesn't seem impressed. "It's perfectly fine to quote. I like to quote, I like to be under the influence of others. It does not cancel out the originality."

"Not all of us are rich and great. You will actually find a lot of originality on the Internet," Andy said.

This time I really didn't want to, but I had to be sarcastic. "Do you know what smaller companies do? They write a song that really reminds people of a popular one, but not exactly. Let's call a spade a spade: That's stealware. We are all in stealth mode here. And do you know what the funniest part is? Companies invest millions upon millions—not in order to create something original of their own, but to steal legally."

"You are my number one trap-maker," Andy replies and elaborates: "I'm not saying this to flatter you. I say this because today I know that then, fifteen years ago, when I was looking for people, professionals or even friends—I was looking for exactly this. I didn't know then that this was what I was looking for. Today I know it is. You have this originality, and whether you connect with yourself, here in Los Gigantes or back home—you will eventually end up in the same place."

It's already late. I feel a little exhausted. Close, but far away. "Is it darkest before dawn? That's what Thomas Fuller wrote in 1650. I remember you liked his work. I know it's not true, but it's very masochistic. Sometimes you have to feel you are in a bit of a crisis, and that the burden is heavier precisely because you are very close to a solution. It looks like you are close." Andy seems confident and I really want to believe him.

"Do you have a free morning or afternoon?"

"I'm flying tomorrow night, so the answer is yes."

"Then I suggest you come with me to meet a friend. I like the way she thinks. She really helped me understand my place here. Give her a chance."

We exchange numbers. Andy sends me to a restaurant on the road to Teide, promising an unforgettable view.

I return to my casa. Santiago and Lucia's stories warmed my heart. It's lovely to see a couple like them, who've been running a unique, authentic place for forty years. A spot that clings to the landscape as well as the land.

In bed, just before falling asleep, I surf the internet in search of their restaurant. I find it on a website for restaurant recommendations. Nice, I think. I curl up deep in the blanket and scroll down the page. "Terrible. They demanded I pay two euros just to use the bathroom," wrote one visitor. "The service is awful, the food is bad." "The landlord is lazy. How are they not ashamed to take so much money from tourists? Don't stop there." "They charge twice as much for rabbit stew as the restaurant next door. Warning—crooks."

Tourist trap? Is this real? Is this the review of an actual tourist who was there? Competitors from the village who are more competent with technology? Maybe Santiago and Lucia just don't know their way around social media?

Chapter 19

I get up on my next-to-the-last morning here. It rained all night. It's almost 50 degrees outside. Windy. I pack my things. I sail out in a car that glides like an island of heat between the drops.

As promised, I show up in the late morning at the Mirador de Chirche. A café-restaurant overlooks the landscape, about a thousand feet below the road that leads up to the Teide Vilaflor reserve at 3,000 feet above sea level.

Andy meets me in the parking lot and, with his umbrella, leads me to the magnificent lookout, made of stone. Most of the tables outside the small restaurant are wet. We sit inside, at a table by the window, and look out. The view features the mountain slope dotted with little hamlets enmeshed in greenery, colorful houses and the beach pouring into the endless ocean.

A few minutes later, a woman in sunglasses with a helmet and a bicycle enters the place. She's wearing long skinny black pants made of breathable fabric with a dark pink stripe. A yellow cycling jersey is loaded with side pockets and a zipper in front. The wheels of her road bike tick to a gentle rhythm. Her feet click with the metal clips that latch onto the pedals. She leans the bike on one of the walls and takes off her helmet and sunglasses. She lets down her light brown hair. "This is Ramagua," Andy introduces her to me. She smiles, reaches out to shake my hand and says she's pleased to meet me.

"Nice meeting you too. I've ridden road bikes for years, but I'm not sure I've reached your level of skill," I say after letting go of her hand.

Andy gives her a long hug. She strokes his back up and down and then kisses him on the cheek, one pace away from his mustache. She is a little wet from the bits of rain.

"Are you having breakfast? Because I'm really hungry after all this uphill pedaling."

"Of course."

We sit at a round table. Andy signals three breakfasts to the waitress. We're here alone. The bored waitress seemed happy to start some activity.

"Andy told me that you are very interested in the history of the island." Ramagua starts off the conversation.

I'm trying to think of how to answer politely without insulting the guest, because that's not exactly what Andy suggested yesterday.

"I thought the history of the island would be of great interest to him, as well as a few other things," Andy intervenes in a politically-something formulation of the purpose of the meeting.

"Gladly," she says. Our coffees arrive, and some almond cookies are placed next to them on the table. "I'm really passionate about explaining to anyone who wants to listen. Naturally, the first human settlers on this island were seafarers."

She seems accustomed to presenting the main points of things and does not wait for my questions. "Researchers believe it goes as far back as the Phoenicians, who were seafarers and traders thousands of years ago. They came to the Canary Islands for the first time so that they would have a mooring spot. A port in their route to trading with Africa, for example. Later, these became the people of Carthage." She sips her coffee and takes a bite from a warm Spanish pastry.

"This was so until the birth of Christianity, more or less, and the end of Carthage age. Some claim that during this period there was a short break of several decades or perhaps a century, after which settlement was resumed, and from there the era of the Guanches began."

I'm still at the listening-and-intellectual-curiosity stage. "OK. Where were they from?"

"Probably Morocco. In any case, from the Berber tribes, who arrived here a little after the beginning of the Christian era. They realized that there was excellent land here, the possibility of developing a port for transporting equipment and supplies, and fantastic weather."

"Just like that, by chance? Why here?" I wondered.

"It is assumed that these tribes received the information from traders and seafarers. Don't forget that the Berbers are tribes descended from the cradle of mankind in Africa, but mixed with Phoenicians and Greeks. You know there are people here who have had DNA tests done to identify their Guanche roots? I met someone whose Guanche stories and souvenirs have been passed down from generation to generation for hundreds of years. You know, like when someone tells you about an investment opportunity only they have? So the same person told me about such a story that goes on in their family from the parent to child. Their ancestors were sailors, ship owners.

"Some shipowners spread a rumor about the fertile island awaiting across the sea, a relatively short voyage of five hundred nautical miles from Marrakech. It is a very difficult trip due to strong sea currents. Still, families and individuals who heard about the opportunity were interested and bought tickets by lottery or on a first-come, first-served basis. I can picture a sunny day when everyone gathered with their gear after paying a hefty fee to the ship's owners to get on board and set sail. Can you imagine such a thing?"

I pause a bit and then let out a short laugh: "Every line has a story."

"As soon as these new settlers engaged in cultivating the land and herding sheep, the whole business developed in a different direction. The Guanches were hunter-gatherers and lived a lifestyle somewhat reminiscent of the Stone Age. It is known they lived in caves and huts and used few tools. Without metals, since they lived on volcanic islands where there are no metal ores. However, they made pottery and had knowledge of basic agriculture and foraging in the wilderness. They also embalmed their dead and their animals inside the caves they inhabited. Then suddenly a tradition began, some crops worked well with the soil and there was contact with international sea traders who came and stopped at the bays. A kind of export and trade."

"Self-determination," I mutter to myself.

"Quite a few excavations have been conducted here. They've unearthed skeletons and physical evidence of villages. Archaeological. There are many charming legends within the Guanche religion. The volcanoes that continuously erupted were an excellent setting for such myths."

We are served some hot pastries. I taste one and offer Andy the plate. "No thanks," he says, "I don't eat meat."

"You? A vegetarian? Andy, you're a fur trader." I'm surprised. Inside the pastry, by the way, there is a little rabbit meat. For the taste, as the waitress points out.

"I learned to separate business from personal life and, as you know, I'm no longer in the business anyway."

"Do you know this man's history?" I turn to Ramagua out of a desire to lighten the atmosphere and also try to assess how the two are connected. "You have a legend here. A dealer in furs, weapons and elephant tusks, who became a vegetarian and talks to me about philosophy."

She nods. "Wait," I say, trying to steer the conversation in another direction, "before the legends—how do you two even know each other?"

"I met Andy at a less good time in his life. I'm allowed to say that, right Andy?" Her brown eyes widen. Small wrinkles appear underneath, and on the sides towards her hair.

"Ramagua met me at the exact time I told you about yesterday," Andy says, taking another sip of his coffee. "We've had many long conversations and special moments together."

"So where did you meet?" I ask again, still not daring to ask if they are a couple. Their behavior is not unambiguous. Both are over fifty, that's clear. Andy sits close to her, almost touching.

"In a pub? In the supermarket? In the street? Andy, did you sell her any fur?"

"You could say that our first encounter wasn't exactly a positive one," replies Ramagua. "A kind of collision between two worlds." That I can imagine.

"The truth is," Andy lowers his gaze a little, "that she crashed into my car." He says it almost with hesitation.

I try to contain my surprise. "Did you crash your car?"

"Back then I got into many fights or just was in a bad mood. I didn't know why. I would get up, take the keys to the BMW and drive away. Anywhere. Just racking miles up on the island. Getting off the main roads, going up into the mountains. My driving was not particularly prudent."

He looks back up and continues: "You realize that Tenerife is a paradise for triathletes. There are a lot of people who come here every year to ride, run and swim—or to do all three."

Ramagua naturally takes the narrator's baton, as if they were co-hosts on a television show. "You can see the signs scattered around the island: 'Caution, cyclists.' Those triangles. I was riding up one of the winding roads not far from here, and down another way, but I was being careful. My gaze was very focused, as it usually is when I'm returning from the mountains, but unfortunately not enough."

"In hindsight I know I was daydreaming. That my mind wasn't there for a few moments. The car swerved and I didn't even stop. I completely ignored the rules, and Ramagua crashed her bike on my front hood." His voice trembles. Like it just happened. As he spoke, his breathing rose and fell noticeably.

He lowered his gaze again. Ramagua slowly placed a gentle hand on his shoulder, leaving it there for a minute or two until Andy calmed down. I had never seen him like that. He was always the confident one. Even in the most difficult crises. He was the one who always said one has to go all the way. Push the limits so the limits don't push you.

"I was very lucky. My bike hit the front grill of the car, and I probably yanked the brakes a little too hard. The bike flew up to the hood and I landed on the windshield instead of rolling to the back of the vehicle, which would have probably crippled me for life."

As opposed to Andy, Ramagua speaks in a calm, trusting tone. While I listen to her account, my gaze locks on her hand still resting on his shoulder. A soothing hand that calms an agitated man reliving his encounter with potential death.

For a moment, just for a moment, I saw Lake's hand resting on my shoulder. It was at the onset of the disease. He leaned on me for a moment as he changed clothes at the hospital. I was shaking a little and tried to hide it as much as I could. I held my hands together, changed the position in the chair. I always wondered if he felt that.

"Just as he smashed me," Ramagua continues speaking openly, "he also saved me."

Almost in unison they tell me that the tenant in the house next door called the police. He told the officer how Andy rammed wildly on their door with his shoulder, how when they opened it, they saw a man carrying an injured woman in his arms. "I have no idea where I got my strength from. I'm not particularly fit. I had a potbelly. I almost fell over when I stepped inside their house," Andy recalls with emotion.

"At the hospital I wanted to tell my friends that this was a knight-saves-princess story, but what kind of knight races with his dragon down the middle of the road and crushes the princess?" Ramagua continues.

"And that's nothing. While Ramagua was undergoing rehab so she could walk again and recover from her wounds, she actually took care of me just as much," Andy completes her and this time I notice his gaze, the way he looks at her. "The first time I went to visit her, mainly out of shame. A nagging conscience. I don't know, I told myself it was for the insurance report. I didn't even notice how I started coming to visit her in the hospital and at rehab more and more frequently. Sometimes I helped her with physical therapy, sometimes we went out to the terrace together and always talked at length.

"Do you get it? Forgive me if I sound corny, ok? But there are things that happen naturally to you. Not under pressure. Without searching for them. Without meaning them to happen. It happened to me. A year. A year and a half, two years. It took me two years to realize that she was my soulmate. We just talked about things. Like a magnet. More and more things. Conversations that turned from small talk to longer ones. Deeper ones."

This is so unlike Andy. "Wow, I'm truly surprised, I must confess." I say it in English, because I don't mind her hearing it too. "You've told me about the Gigantes that restored your peace and about how you two got together. I'm really happy for you and glad to meet you, Ramagua. But you asked me to come here following our conversation, and I don't quite understand how it's all related."

I'm beginning to lose my patience. I try to bring it back through a bite of one of the pastries that is still warm. The windows are frosted due to the temperature differences. On the opposite wall of the restaurant far from me, some wood is burning in the fireplace.

"You can say it's a kind of realization. Maybe even a sort of ideology," Ramagua says. "We would be walking in the hospital or out for a moment in the cafeteria, and find ourselves talking about it. About the restlessness in both of us."

"And in the meantime," Andy completes her line of thought again, "Ramagua began to take a deep interest in her Guanche roots." I thought he was changing the subject. The Guanche roots are not together. They might be hers, but certainly not his.

Ramagua now takes over in a quiet, relaxed and comforting speech. She looks at me with understanding eyes. My body relaxes a little. "During rehab, I decided that this would be my post-doctorate thesis. My father told me stories about his ancestors when I was still lying in the hospital unable to move very much. I admit that at forty-five I was more attracted by this than at twenty-five.

"It's like a stew, maybe a root-vegetable soup," she smiles for a moment. "His stories, my roots. The restlessness we both felt. My dad's stories about Los Gigantes—I sent Andy there. It all converged into one thing that I can't even name. Some ideology."

"Excuse me," I jump on her, as if I had been waiting with a catapult to shoot my answer. "After so many years in advertising, I can assure you—there is no ideology. There might be *Weedology*. That means doing everything to get whatever brings you a little weed just for laughs or to gain more time somewhere. Like a game of musical chairs. To capture another percentage of market share that someone else will grab back with their next campaign."

Now my patience is really running out. "Let me take a wild guess—in those years a lot of people discovered their roots here and it became sort of a movement."

"That's not untrue," Andy says. "But sometimes things just fall into place together. So what? So what if there was a trend? What interests me is what suits me. Who cares what other people think? Everything worked out well for me. Ramagua. Our conversations. The fact that she connected with her roots. Granted, it took me two years, but it worked out fine. Why resist it if it's so good?"

"Listen, you match-made-in-heaven love doves," I say with sarcasm, starting with a firm statement and ending with the space found between a question mark and an exclamation mark, not letting my body relax. The mind strongly resists this psychological intervention imposed on me, like someone is hypnotizing you, but you resist. Like in a thriller.

"An accident, hard as it may have been, is one thing, and I truly wish you all the best in the world." Pomposity takes over me, lengthening my words here and there, playing with them in exaggeration. "But can you even understand what's going on?"

I can hardly control what I'm being overwhelmed with, but I try my best. I stop for a moment, because I notice that I'm almost shouting. I push the volume down and try to go on. "Everything fell apart for me. My boy died. He's dead. He grew up, matured, and became a wonderful young man, full of kindness. A unique person. Then he fell ill and died all at once. No early signs, no risk factors. He withered right before my eyes, and there was nothing I could do about it."

Andy looks at Ramagua. She looks back at him, the corners of her mouth crinkle.

Two riders enter the restaurant, a young man and woman, soaked to the bone. One of their bicycle wheels is punctured. They speak English with a heavy Texan accent. They ask for hot drinks and sit down by the fireplace. They immediately hold hands, kiss passionately. They're elated by the adventure of riding up the road, the steep gradients, the pouring rain and the intimacy created by a joint effort next to each other, sometimes just a meter apart. Wrapped in helmets, glasses, shields and thermal clothes. The passion of a man and a woman in their twenties.

They share hot drinks and watch an episode of a drama series playing at low volume on the TV screen on the wall. "I'm sorry, this is not a social visit," says the man in the series to the young woman with whom he is sitting at a bar. "I asked my boss to be the one to tell you, because I am your uncle." His face is filled with sorrow. "David is no longer alive. He isn't missing, he's dead." Upon hearing his words, the young woman bursts into heartbreaking tears and collapses into his arms.

"Andy, Ramagua," I say, looking at them with my elbows on the table. "In the past year I've watched more suspense series than I had in my entire life. Except recently, every time something sad happens, like someone is in pain, a terrible truth is revealed, or there is a tragic story about a young person on the evening news—I just fall apart. I cry. My emoti-meter is out of whack. How can you live like this? What formulas and ideologies are you talking about?"

"Obviously," Ramagua tries saying, "one can't compare." It is clear to me that they both mean to help, but perhaps they fell upon a task that is too big for them. The happiness notebook I brought with me to write something down if I feel the need is open on the table. "My conclusion right now is that there are no conclusions. That so far everything has failed, and maybe the only thing I take from here, Andy, is that if I manage to find a way to make a living working remotely, maybe I'll settle down in Masca, simply because there I was able to find a little more peace than in other places."

"I'm just saying," Ramagua rephrases, "personally, I was going through a very bad period in my life when it happened. I may have even punished myself without knowing it. I was traumatized too. After a difficult divorce, a doctorate that I barely finished that dragged out for years and having to move back in with my parents because I had no way of earning enough to have my own home. So was Andy, as you realized.

"But... how do I explain to you what I want to say? I want to tell you there's a happy ending, but that's not accurate. It is not the end and the word happy doesn't fit here. Maybe it's the next segment of the road, but that's not accurate either. More like the stew that works for you. I'm trying to find the words."

Andy gets up from the table. "Do you remember when we submitted the appeal to the Supreme Court?" He waves both hands as if there was a cloak behind him.

"Sure."

"After the judge sent a message, a strong hint that the state should reach a settlement with us so that he does not rule against them, we sat in the court cafeteria. For an hour we talked with that big, tall, broad-shouldered lawyer. Eventually we reached an agreement. He left the premises and we celebrated with Coke, coffee and wafers."

"I remember," I reply dryly.

"I asked our lawyer how all that was necessary. After all, the state knew we were right on that article of the law. Why did we have to go through all that agony? Remember I asked?"

"I remember," again I say impatiently.

"I apologize for using the word agony. I know it's not the most appropriate expression at the moment," he tries to lighten it up, but I don't relent. "Anyway, it's not like I was overjoyed. There were many more challenges, but still, a ray of light appeared and there was a feeling of optimism."

"Yes, yes. I remember all of it. So what are you trying to say?" I got up from the table, strode towards the window and came back.

"The lawyer told me that there is no such thing, that we must go through this process. That's how it is. It has to be. Because everyone has to go through it. Otherwise it doesn't work. The frustration, the fighting, the appeals. What did Ramagua say? Stew? I'll adopt this metaphor. The stew must be burned. Maybe you even need a few lousy dishes before you can learn to cook. How am I at metaphors? Huh?" He smiles, waves a hand and pats me on the back. "Or sad stews in order to be happy at the end? But we must first cook the sad ones. We must. Then you have to hope the circumstances will line up and mingle so that the right ingredients are cooked. It's all a matter of ingredients and what one does with them."

That was one joke too many for me. Everything inside me is boiling. My mind and my body refuse to participate in this feast of excessive logic. I pick up the happiness notebook and wave it. "But I want to be sad," I shout in my mother tongue, and the whole restaurant hall hears me. "I don't want to be happy, or discover moments of happiness, or cook any dishes." The notebook of happiness falls and opens, face down. "I don't want to forget any sad picture. I want my heart to keep shrinking every day," I say returning to English. Now I'm banging hard on the table, completely oblivious to the fact that I'm in the middle of a restaurant. The couple in love looks at me. The waitress cringes, maybe trying to disappear a little.

My voice starts to tremble. I hold my head in my hands.

"I know," Ramagua says. She doesn't make any effort at all to stop my volcanic eruption, the bubbling magma spewing out of me. She seems to accept it.

"So how can it be that I both must go back there all the time and also want to forget it all the time? To get up tomorrow morning with a new song in my heart but also to stab my heart?" I sit back down. A few tears run down the side of my cheeks. I rest my head gently on the arms that are crossed on the table.

Ramagua places her hand on mine. "I have a story for you. Every summer a large part of the Guanche residents, men, women and children from all over the island would abandon their settlements in the mid-altitude region of the island, between the arid coast and the mountains, leaving behind their mild climate and abundant water streams, and climb the mountains to spend a few months in small shelters made of stone."

I raise my head and listen to her, wiping my tears. "They didn't go on holiday. They took their herds of goats with them. They didn't have the equipment we do. No one arranged for them any hydration packs, thermal dry fit clothes, or hiking shoes. Yet they survived. They climbed up the Teide because there were fresh plants there. Sometimes people died there. Did not survive. When the Spaniards invaded and launched their attack to conquer the island, the Guanche fled to the mountain. To those same places. To hide in the caves."

"Everything gets mixed together," Andy says. "I feel it.

How hardship and pain become fertile ground for something good, and how that good something sometimes hurts and reminds us of the trauma of the past. How the shelter can be a very difficult place to hide in, but there is something protective about it despite the difficulties. It's not that we are always so cheerful and happy. We only managed to understand and accept the journey. And also with the time it takes. Your time is coming too. You had to go through all of this, and there are no shortcuts."

I feel suffocated. Ignoring the weather outside, I try to push the door open, but the wind is strong. I use all my strength and go out to the terrace. The drops fall on my head, pounding like many small hammers pressed together. Streams form on my coat and run down from me to the floor. I take another step under the umbrella that is meant to provide shade from the sun, not to protect from rain. It is on the verge of being torn off, held in place only by a concrete casting that encases its base. The rain flies at me diagonally. I'm cold. I place my foot on a large stone at the end of the path. The edge of the concrete terrace, which is one step ahead, is cut almost ninety degrees downwards.

Again the phone rings and doesn't stop. I dip my hand in my pocket, pull out my cell phone and hold tight to the wind. God's assistant. I decide to click. Maybe we'll just put an end to that too and leave it behind me. "Hello," I say loudly, almost shouting. As if we were talking through the cups of a string telephone and not on our mobiles on both sides of the ocean. "Hey, I'm sorry to disturb you on your holiday, but..." she says and I could maybe hear the rest, but I don't. The rain wets my cell phone and my head. The steep cliffs make me dizzy. She says something about an event and a problem and 'urgent' and that God is not willing to wait any longer for me to return His calls.

"I am so-rry," I shout again, pronouncing each syllable, like we are at a party, "I can't hear that well." Hail mixed with rain floods a percussion orchestra into the foyer, which is full of polished stones and tables that look like they won't be able to withstand it all. "And something must be done about it. He wants to discuss it," she finishes the sentence. I turn up the volume on the phone all the way but I still can't hear.

"So what do we do?" I shout again, and I don't mean her at all. "What do we do?" I try in vain to take in a little more scenery to lower my heart rate, but it only gets stronger. The landscape and the rain and the mountains and the sea just call me to come closer to them. Maybe one or two more steps forward will do it. I consider whether I want to live or die. What would happen if I jumped over the edge and ended all of this? Uniting with the wild landscape, becoming part of the rock and soil.

I let the wind sway me. Let it decide. Maybe it'll just blow me off the terrace, and it'll be an unfortunate accident. I yell at God's assistant: "Fuck off. Go to hell together with all the crap I have to pick up after you." The mobile phone flies off my hand and becomes stuck at the bottom of the rockery that separates me from the abyss. My foot trips over the rock.

Chapter 20

Andy and Ramagua surprise me from behind. I didn't notice them following me. Andy grabs me by the hem of my clothes. They ask if I'm okay, trying not to startle me. Holding me gently, they take down my raised hand. Ramagua wraps me in an unexpected hug, like a shaman or a healer. Andy pulls my body slowly backwards. He picks up the phone that was trapped in the corner of the rockery. They gently steer me back towards the restaurant.

The door slams shut from the force of the wind and we are inside. Back in the warm womb, with the burning hearth. We sit back down at the table. Andy asks for a large pot of hot tea and pours it for us.

"I'm not saying it has to happen tomorrow morning, but can I hope to wake up in a year, or in two, and know that I'm done with it? That it shall pass? That something new will begin? That I have put a period, and can breathe again?"

"There is no period. A dot is something we humans invented so we can communicate with others. It's up to us. There is no period. There is no comma. We stop and break chains of ideas, of stories, but none of it is real. There is no such a thing as an end, nor are there periods. You don't really start anything. You only take over and continue. All the time. Nothing disappears and everything is built on the foundations of something else," Ramagua says, throwing everything on the table. Without mercy.

"I sometimes wake up at night and think about all the animals that were killed because of me, and maybe also humans. I've been here for a long time. I have a good life. I sometimes write down memories of places I visited when I was a trader. Remote corners of Africa. We are a storehouse of emotions that arise in us as a result of everything we've been through. It sits there. It will rise like yeast. Most of the time it stays hidden, but sometimes it seeps out. No event that you experienced is ever completely left behind."

"Everyone hopes for a happy ending, an ending where the princess is saved, marries the prince, and they live happily ever after. Catharsis. Aren't you in catharsis?" After feeling like a huge wave crashing against the Los Gigantes cliffs, my heart grew tired, drifted to the safe harbor at the bottom of the big black rocks, and sought to lie still, to let go, and hope for the best.

"It won't pass and the void will always be there, I guess. For me, at least, it was like soil fertilizer. The moment I almost ceased to be here made me investigate, search, and persevere. It made my discovery more tangible, more immense, more precious. It didn't happen to me consciously. It happened gradually," Ramagua purses her lips and then relaxes them into a small, conciliatory smile.

Ramagua approaches the young couple and addresses them. "May I suggest that, as long as you're here, you enjoy the Guanche spirit? It'll do a lot of good for your relationship. We have an awesome series of workshops in the mountains and even a Guanche residence you can subscribe to, and come twice a year to breathe air you won't breathe anywhere else." They say they'll think about it and she returns to her seat.

"I hardly know you, I don't know this place, and maybe that's the advantage. I think I allowed myself to do here what I couldn't bring myself to do for the last two years. I just want to understand how I can live with all of this."

"You live. You live a little more each time." Andy's voice rises and falls like a little siren alarm. Then he pulls out a pen and draws concentric circles on a napkin, like those mazes next to the crossword puzzles. "Yes," he says as he makes an exciting discovery, while examining what he scribbled. "It's like you're a satellite in a spiral orbit. Like a snail. You discover things that touch you, both the bad and the painful, but also the good, and they suddenly move you very much. Something in your whole body becomes more sensitive. As if someone rewired the scale," he said, placing his non-drawing hand on Ramagua's.

"And sometimes the trajectory brings you back into the pain, a bit like a meteor hitting Earth." You have to be careful not to get burned by it. It sears a valley in your body. A crater. But then you launch yourself like a rocket, or like one of those satellites, from the crater to the moon, far into the distance, and yesterday's pain becomes the fuel of your life tomorrow."

"You're quite the poet." This time I take the role of lightening things up, trying to smile. A skeptical smile that doesn't buy all that. My hair is still dripping.

I get up and pace back and forth in the restaurant. The heat emitted from the hot fireplace floods the hall. The young couple already paid and left and we are alone again, because it is raining a lot now and tourists don't go out in such weather. The windows are all fogged up.

"Come, stay here with us. It will do you good." Ramagua gathers all her skill into a gaze, a body language. Eyes one can't resist. I look at them for a long time.

"You're talented," he says finally. "I know you. I need someone like you with us. You are a true professional. Tourists grab our workshops and accommodations in the mountains like there is no tomorrow. And we do it with love. Look how awesome and peaceful it is here. You will feel calm," Andy says to me with the tenderness of a caring father.

"You've always been full of shit, Andy. The same trick I fall for every time. Your charm, your charisma. Your ability to sell anything to anyone, as if it were infinite goodness, even when it's a weapon for a tribe in Africa. You sell it like you're with the good guys. And there, you've fooled me all over again. I almost fell for it. You saw the light, and now you feel the need to reveal it to everyone else."

I bend down to pick up my happiness notebook, turn a page and start drawing.

"There is no period," I echo Ramagua. In my language, not in English. I look at Andy's snail, think about the spiral and the satellite, and eventually I draw another satellite orbit. I reroute the pen in a circle that intersects and turns into a second circle. A horizontal eight. Infinity. No end.

Chapter 21

Explosion

For a few years, after I joined my first advertising agency, I still heard the loud knocks on the door. The shouting and the dogs. And the huge explosion. I heard them in a different way.

I would be taking a nap on a Friday afternoon, falling asleep at the beach or watching a TV series late at night, gnawing on a pizza and dozing off, and they would barge into the dream. Combat in an urban area that scrolls into a small room with a steel door. The explosion of grenades echoing through the air. At the exact tempo of those knocks, the rap of the barking dogs. But in Grenadese. And I am helpless. Trapped. In excruciating pain. Trembling.

A dream about celebrating Independence Day. Men and women like me, dancing, drinking. I click with one of the women. We progress from the dance floor to the bathroom. While we're fucking, someone knocks loudly on the toilet door. Drunken men demand that I open. The sound is different, but the tempo is the same as before. I thrust my body back and forth, and as I turn my head, I see the door being shaken violently, about to break open any second. I'm terrified.

I play my electric guitar with a large amp. I devote my whole self to music, and suddenly other voices are added to the distortion. Kicks and screams twist the sound, convulsing the airwaves. They rattle the membrane of the speaker from the inside out. The muffle becomes bass. It threatens to tear the fabric, cardboard and wood that make up the speaker.

In every dream, something would eventually erupt and run me over, trampling me to mush. A bulldozer, a gigantic pair of shoes, horses, fifteen-foot tall hammers. And while I was being tormented, chopped into a thousand pieces in complete helplessness, I screamed, shrieked, choked, suffocated—but nothing happened. I couldn't get a peep out of my throat. Until I woke up, shaking and sweaty.

* * *

It was my very last day of arranging the paperwork at the university. A few weeks after my dad's funeral. I was a young man getting his diploma and transcript of grades. I settled my debt at the library and had a coffee with a friend. I took a last look at the auditoriums, classrooms and halls.

Towards seven, I went to the Midtown branch on the pedestrian mall. I came to help with various errands, as my mother requested. The broad man was in the front, as usual, talking to vendors, yelling at the merchandiser, a new hiree who was replenishing the spirits shelf in the corner farthest from the entrance. He then shouted that he was going to do store checks in all the branches.

Mom was on the second floor, above the store. As

usual, she sat there looking impressive with her impeccable make-up and a floral-patterned dress. In fact, I don't remember her in homewear or without her makeup on. Dad used to call her the Secretary of State. Even when I was a toddler playing at home, or as a little boy, Mom was always neatly dressed. Perfectly groomed.

She also fulfilled this role in the days preceding and following Dad's funeral. Every morning she welcomed the guests in a black dress, and exuded the scent of citrus fruits. The house was polished clean and brimming with refreshments brought from the store. Our partners continued to run the shops, as usual, while Mom presided over a royal diplomatic ball where guests were received one by one. I sat there with a polite face, in a white shirt that she demanded I wear, dark pants and black shoes, with my hair properly combed.

The beams of our modest living room grew in my imagination into porticos decorated with luxurious curtains. Mona, an employee of many years, was sent to help, acting as a waitress circulating among the arrivals. Bubbles and fizzes that were too cheerful for the doleful mood, devoured the liquid poured from bottles of Cola Funola and Lemony FunFizz produced by the *So Refreshing* company. Life is a wheel. Once the fat man asked, referring to this soda: "How much bleach should I order from the So Refreshing factory?" and suggested we use it to mop the floor. Of course, never in front of the customers who bought a liter-and-a-half bottle for ninety-nine cents, when our buying cost was less than twenty cents. During the days of mourning, we poured that drink into tall, narrow plastic glasses like champagne.

Through the open door came the mayors of the

surrounding towns where our branches were located. Suppliers, large customers, heads of PTA's, and directors of retirement homes also came. Figures about whom the local gossip sections wrote: "Seen at..." or "Married the love of his life on..." and "Spotted in..." Sometimes they wore suits and sometimes t-shirts and jeans. Mom welcomed all of them with hugs and kisses, with words that came from the heart and her thirst for their words about my dad's wonders.

These ceremonies were my hugging academy. I analyzed them, studied them. I saw my mom embracing the director of the *Partying Patients* association, who used to buy candy and balloons from us to hand out on their visits to hospitals. I saw the movement of her right hand on his, while her left hand rested on his shoulder for a moment. The kiss with a slight tilt to the left of the face and the puckering of the lips towards his cheek. Her body leaning forward a little and showing excessive affection. I studied her inquisitive "Hmm," the slight nod of the head. When her hair was gathered, she would shake it.

Throughout my childhood and adolescence, all this was drowned out in the flow of life, seen here and there. But in the mourning reception bootcamp, the high concentration provided overwhelming insights. It dawned on me for the first time that there was no difference between them and me. That's the way my mom hugged me when I was three years old and I fell off the swing. Like that, with the slight movement of the head, she asked me if I was OK. I felt I knew that already a long time ago. Business. Not necessarily pleasure.

When all the condolences were over, Mom rushed out to the chain's headquarters located near the pedestrian mall in Midtown, maintaining the same grandeur. She continued to walk every day with her hair gathered. Clicking her heels, wearing a necklace. The old houses in the small streets are decades old. The tenants of some of the apartments were prostitutes, drug addicts and petty thieves. There were smelly trash cans, sewage juices flowing here and there. Most of the time she skipped to the second floor after a brief "Hi" at the store. She sometimes patrolled the other branches in our black Volvo.

Since I was a baby I was left to the care of a nanny and then kindergarten. My mom left early on to help promote dad's business. The same was true that evening, when I went up to the second floor of the building. I wanted to tell her that I was done with philosophy. I had a degree. But when I opened the door and she saw me, she immediately said: "Come. I need your help. I'm drowning in these calculations." The tone of her voice was motherly and tender but also purposeful.

"Mom, I told you, I know how to help you with the calculations like dad taught me, but I'm not an expert at it. I don't know all the rules. Shouldn't you sit with the accountant? With our bookkeeper?"

"It's not that complicated," she replied.

I sighed and dragged a chair next to hers. The computer screen displayed lots of tables and numbers from the accounting software.

"Look, something here in the balance sheet doesn't add up." Her fingernails, anointed with pink polish, strolled delicately on the screen.

Since my dad passed away I tried to focus on my thesis at the university. I helped with chores in our stores, but I tried to do everything to keep up in the race and finally obtain my degree. I immersed myself in Descartes, Wittgenstein, Putnam, Bergson.

Mom asked me to deepen my involvement in the business. "You know numbers and you have good ideas," she reasoned. "Dad always said you had good ideas—ideas for how to make money, how to name things, how to write things."

I tried to delve into the monitor. Dad really encouraged me in every way to 'enter the business.' In a vote of confidence in my abilities, at the age of twelve he bought me a ten-gear bicycle and suggested I run errands for him, for which he paid me handsome pocket money. At first, I rode between the branches in the towns within my realm. I did my leisurely rounds between the stores, carrying on my back goods that needed to be delivered, taking cash deposits to the bank, checks or important mail that had to reach Dad.

Later on, when I was about thirteen, he shared with me the bills, the orders and the journal entries. He taught me to read the numbers, to understand financial logic. I became excited with the printing calculator on his desk. Dad saw this and told me he would test me in two months' time on numbers and accounting. If I passed it, I could get my own calculator.

I did. In my room at home I sat and ticked off numbers that turned into small metal levers that burst into a frenzy, numbers that were etched like a tattoo into the paper that suffered everything in silence. It surprised and excited me at the same time. I looked at the product, looking for the logic of the numbers, but found something else in them. Very quickly my gaze wandered from the paper roll to the small monitor. I dismantled in my mind the vertical and horizontal lines that made up the digits, and time after time I practiced digits that would turn into words and shapes.

I waved the baton in the calculators' Independence Day parade, I wrote down on a separate sheet the numbers I checked, and then I ran them again like in a dress rehearsal. I ended by waving a flag—that is with a roll of paper trailing under the table like a bride's train.

But that evening it was already long after the calculator. The street lights indicated the lateness of the hour. Mom tapped a fingernail on the monitor. "Are you listening? Look what's going on here. Maybe you want me to print these ledger cards for you?"

I nodded, trying to act like someone who understands the subject. She hesitated for a moment, then began tapping a few shortcuts, sending the results to a printer on a shelf. Once Dad allowed me to leave on that shelf the book I was reading at the time.

Ever since I was a little boy, my dad knew I read the books that lay in piles by my bed. Books I borrowed from the public library. He said it wasn't a bad thing. One had to know how to read, but it was better not to overdo it. It was a fragile deal. Because one day, when I was seven, I went into my room. I reached for my desk which consisted of a writing surface with a set of drawers and shelves, and pulled it forward a little. I leaned into the back of it and, to my astonishment, my secret drawer had been broken into. It was a small wooden rear drawer that I locked with a small padlock I brought from one of Dad's stores without his knowledge. I thought no one knew about the drawer but, just to be safe, I locked it.

At the age of four I discovered the corner with the

heavy, colorful books at my kindergarten. The ones with lots of pictures and lots of words. The ones that smelled so good, with the same smell as when Dad stopped to fill up gas. Then a fire was lit in my body. Not a bonfire that burns. A campfire that stays warm and bright thanks to pictures and letters.

It took me a while to figure out the name of the book. It was written on the hard bright-red cover. *Encyclopedia for Children.* I flipped through the pages. Whenever I found a beautiful picture that I really liked, of a flower or a man or a tower, I tried to read the scripture as much as I could. A man called Pasteur. A tower called Pisa. A flower named snapdragon. If I didn't get a word, I would ask the kindergarten teacher. I didn't want to say anything to my parents. I also asked Monica who often sat next to me in the play corner of the school. I knew she was smart by her eyes, and also because I asked her the hardest questions and she always knew the answers. The letters and the illustrations merged together. The letter 'E' looked like a comb, and became a table when turned on its side.

Then my inner word machine kicked in. I found myself taking sheets of paper and scribbling words on them until my hand hurt. *Where do I put all these words?* I asked myself. I thought about the book corner at kindergarten. I also wanted to tell Monica that I could write, but I was ashamed. I know she didn't mind that all the kids in the class talked about football, fistfights and TV, and that I didn't. Nor that I wrote with my left hand while everyone else used their right hand. I didn't know anyone, adults or children, who wrote with a different hand. I didn't want her to think there was something wrong with me. I wanted her to stay friends with me.

Eventually I mustered up the courage, but it was only at the age of seven. I was waiting for the right moment for Monica to be with me in the vocabulary room in the classroom, after school hours. I pulled out some papers. I showed them to her. I told her I wrote that. I read to her a paragraph from one of them, about a man with an umbrella who walks in the rain and falls into a puddle. I was shaking. I felt as if I were undressing before a shower in front of everyone. My voice could barely be heard over my heartbeat.

She asked if the man needed help, and suggested I might consider writing about a dog licking him and helping him up. I felt like I was paralyzed, but at the same time I was dancing. I wanted to be close. To talk to her more. Even though I was blushing, even though I was embarrassed. And so our encounters in the word room turned into secret meetings where we shared commentary and added the children of the second grade to the short stories I wrote in my notebook.

One day I sat next to her and we slid a little closer to each other. Then I put my lips on her cheek, like mom sometimes did. Out of the corner of my eye I could see her smiling. At that moment, the teacher walked in. She separated us. She looked at the sheets of paper I was holding in my hand and said nothing. Then there were lectures about it not being allowed. No touching. The pages were confiscated. I didn't know what to do. I began wetting my bed again. I felt I could only write if I hid the pages well.

At first I had the brilliant idea of burying them under the mattress. It helped me avoid wetting the sheet at night. But then I was given the writing desk. I watched in amazement as the carpenter assembled it in my room.

When he left, I discovered the defect. The carpenter unintentionally gapped a space between two pieces at the back, creating a small drawer without a handle. That's how my pages found their home.

But that afternoon, at the age of seven, I stood crying, furious at the sight of the broken, empty drawer. Mom had ordered the cleaner to do a thorough job in my room. When she moved the large desk, she found the drawer, and easily forced the lock. As far as my parents were concerned, these papers had to go straight to the trash. They didn't care about the stolen padlock. They talked about the 'imagination' pages that may make one do bad things again."

From that day on, Dad decided that every day I had off school I would spend in the store. The deal was that he would allow me to read books, he would pay the library subscription fees, but I had to be in the store during all my holidays. And without paper. Without writing. As time went by and the level of boredom increased, I examined the goods in the store, read and made entries on accounting ledgers, and asked questions about suppliers and customers. Dad had the patience to explain it all to me. I told myself that patience is probably a limited thing, like a battery and, according to the law of conservation of energy—if he had a lot of patience for explanations about the business, he had to run out of patience elsewhere. I eagerly used up the patience battery and consumed his words. The positive and the negative. That's how I started coming up with ideas about switching suppliers and finding ways to achieve what I realized years later were higher profit margins.

One summer, Dad took me to the seashore and sat me

down at the beach. He suggested I build sand castles, eat watermelon. Play in the shallow water. Then, when we were resting afterwards, he casually said to me: "I know you remember your written pages. I did it because I wanted to help you."

I blushed in silent embarrassment. "Don't worry, you don't have to say anything," he said. "If you feel that you need, that you want a girl, a young woman. Let's say you need a sort of Monica. So there are ways. I can help you find them. When the time comes, let me know.

"You don't need this nonsense," he continued. "I will teach you what you need to know. A man should be a manager, use his talents. And you are already a man. And if your talent is hindered by all kinds of things, things let's say like you felt then, with the pages you wanted to show the girl in kindergarten. If you feel such things, you need to find other solutions. Solutions that..." He paused for a moment to find the right words, and finally said: "Solutions that will help you stay focused on the important stuff."

The store was already closed. I pored over the materials Mom had printed for me for a long time. I went through them row by row and studied them in depth. Finally, after much effort, I noticed some lines that weren't working for me. I went into the computer and entered a few additional queries, then went through it all again. "Mom, I think I found it," I said to her. "Here is another record of our accounting, shown in a different way. It contained data on Pick-up Sticks, Go Fish cards, and Scattergories. In previous years they yielded very handsome incomes. But in recent months, revenues from these items decreased. In fact, in the last two months they completely disappeared."

Mom's eyes widened as she stared at me. For the first time in my life I saw her go pale. Paler than the moment she learned that Dad had died suddenly. "I do remember that we carry a few games like those, but I didn't know they made up such a significant percentage of our sales." I tried to figure out what my mom's shaking and sweat had to do with what I just said to her.

"Maybe you should go now. I'll wrap things up here. Thanks for your help," she said to me.

Nothing in the picture made any sense to me. I tried to ask her for an explanation. But she did all she could to give me the impression that everything was normal. I didn't buy that, so I told her I'd be right back and went to get a glass of water.

Downstairs in the kitchenette I opened my college transcripts. I went over the list of courses and grades. It was close to midnight. I stared at the window. Previous moments of my life floated up. Minutes later, the silence was disrupted by loud noises from the street. Sounds of a large vehicle screeching to a halt. No one stops by or drives on this street at night. Cars don't just enter a pedestrian mall. I went back to the office room. Several men were causing a racket. Laughing out loud. Dogs barked. One man shouted: "Jonah and Sons and Wife, where are you?"

I saw Mom peeking out the window for an instant, then standing up in a panic. She locked the door from the inside with all the locks, and activated the security systems. "What are you doing? We'll be trapped in here. Do you know these people?" Before I could figure out what was happening, they had walked past the store to the side alley. The voices of men and dogs grew louder, echoing between the rear space adjacent to the shop and the entrance to our stairwell. Mom turned off the light and grabbed my hand. In the corner of the office room was a sewing machine that she used on occasion. She pulled my arm hard, forcing me to squat down with her and crouch under the machine stand, into a small cabinet.

I sat cross-legged on the wide iron pedal, my head bent forward, my hands clasped. Mom joined me in the adjacent compartment, between smaller shelves where the sewing threads were kept. The place was not made to fit two adults shaking with fear. We could only half-close the door. We sat close to each other as tightly as possible. From our hideaway we heard fists beating in tempo on the steel door with the special locking mechanism designed to protect our safe from being robbed. The dogs barked menacingly. The men roared: "Your time is up. You're giving it to us now or you're done. Do you hear? You're finished." The stairwell was filled with screams. The noise of the blows grew louder. From punching to hitting rackets. They knew the neighbors wouldn't call the police.

A moment later we heard the sound of some electrical tool and the door began to rattle. Someone was trying to break in. We were stunned. My mom knew something and I knew nothing. "I get it," screamed one of the voices from within the commotion. "I see what you're up to, lady." The dogs and men drummed their shoes and feet down the stairs. An instant later, something that sounded like a rock hit the door. Seconds later we heard an explosion.

Chapter 22

The Calling

The noise is deafening. The disparity that exists between being silent and screaming. Between the depth of the ocean and a wave crashing against a ship. Between deep sleep in the darkness of the night and bright, sudden daylight. Although the men and dogs only ran downstairs to get away and their voices did not disappear, for me they faded away.

For me, in the seconds before the explosion, absolute silence reigned. The kind that rattled the steel door, whose vibrations turned into a series of thunders through the structure of the building that seemed to be shivering, experiencing thousands of tiny oscillations in a few seconds. It clung on trying to remain whole, devoting all its breath, straining all its muscles to keep the bricks, walls and plaster glued together. Perhaps even panting, as the noise made by our old gutters sounded to me.

We froze in our cramped compartment. Feeling we were shrinking our bodies to a fraction of their size and compressing into ourselves in heaping portions. I shut my eyes and covered my ears, but it was too late. They had already absorbed most of the shock and noise. Then it was quiet again for a few seconds. Maybe thirty. I opened my eyes in the dark. I saw my sweat stains. I saw Mom. Still well-groomed, but frightened, withered. Mature. Older. Aged in an instant. Her dress was also marred by sweat stains. Her hair was disheveled, tangled. Her gaze is neither diplomatic nor welcoming.

Whereas in the nightmares that ensued the doors were always busted open and terror lashed out from them mercilessly, here the men's voices and dog barks subsided. The door barely remained standing, in an incident later reported in the local news as "what appeared to be a warning by criminals using a stun grenade explosion near a Midtown building. At this point, the police don't yet know the identity of the criminals or why the attempt was directed at this particular building."

It was later reported that the police believed there had been a mistake in the address. The message was probably meant for the neighboring building, where there had long been a territorial dispute between two pimps who controlled prostitution and drug trafficking rings in the area.

Finally the men and dogs left. From the cabinet under the sewing machine we clearly heard their car driving away. I crawled out and helped Mom get up. I offered to make her coffee, and suggested we stay for a while. That she not go home right away. That we calm down a little first.

She sat down in the office chair. She agreed to me making coffee for her and waiting a moment before going home. "In any case, it's better to keep everything locked up for a while longer, so they won't find out we were here all this time," she reasoned about the action to be taken.

I made us coffee while trying to process the moments that had just elapsed. The distance between that boy who was so excited to break speed records riding from branch to branch, with the chain of his bike clunking every time he shifted gears. Picking the exact right moment to switch, adjusting the transmission ratio between the wheels to the slope of the road, while my back was loaded with bags or packages. These assignments allowed me to go on reading books about the Nuremberg trials, the history of liberalism, American politics, environmental history. Philosophy for young minds.

When I wanted to trade the bicycle for a motorcycle, my dad smiled. I was already familiar with the stores, the merchandise. I had already suggested ideas for rebranding the chain. Its colors. Fonts. I had already come up with slogans and designed ads. I had offered ideas for packaging tailored to the needs of specific segments of the population.

"Let's do it like men, like businessmen," he suggested. "How about we go out to lunch? You and me." I was overjoyed. We decided on burgers. I parked my bike outside. Local newspapers had been scattered on the tables. With municipal elections six months away, I eagerly devoured every bit of information on politics. I was so engrossed in reading everything, including the gossip, I didn't notice when Dad came in and sat down in front of me. "Interesting," he said, catching me by surprise. "Who do you think will win the town elections?"

"Apparently it seems that Clifford has the highest chances of being elected," I said, "but I think Harold will be the surprise candidate. He will win by just a few votes. And anyway, he will be running the city even if Clifford wins."

A bit taken aback, he asked me to explain. I presented my case. I watched him ingest my words eagerly. My father is learning from me, not I from him. I was bubbling all over with pride. But I didn't stammer or waver. I laid it all out. In a natural manner.

The waiter arrived. Dad didn't ask me what I wanted in my burger. He ordered one for me with all the toppings and one for himself. "I have a deal for you. Like between two businessmen," he said in a somewhat feigned bass tone. But I didn't think he was putting on a show. I felt it was completely genuine. "I'll take care of it. Not a motorcycle, but a car. You are sixteen, soon you'll be allowed to start driving lessons. In the meantime, we will get you a moped license, but only for the time being. Once you learn to drive, you'll get a car from me."

My heart pounded loudly. Past experience had taught me that there would be a price to pay. "What do you want from me? What do you want in return?" I asked.

"I want you to read only about the elections, in the newspapers. In general, read the papers. Read about politics. We have ideas to further expand the chain. Your mother knows how to network. She'll know how to translate your ideas into actions."

It all hit me. I took a few deep breaths, shifted my glance left and right, looking for something to cling to, to keep myself from crying, from being sad, from getting nervous. To avoid showing him that I had no way of leveraging against his will. I had no choice but to agree. I forced my gaze towards the fan across from him. I tried to address it instead of the great man—the arbiter of fate on the other side of the table.

"I also want to be able to read books," I said in a whisper that was barely audible in the hustle and bustle of the after-hours in one of the packed hamburger places in the city. But my dad heard me alright. "Listen, man," he said, "there are only twenty-four hours in a day. Reading your books won't serve any purpose. But if you read the news, you'll be using your mind for a good cause. This is my business logic."

He extended his two large, thick hands towards the bun that lay on its side, open-mouthed, almost knocked out, loaded with all the goodies. I watched his hands above the tray, tightening their grip around the burger. Clamping firmly in order to contain, but not to break, not to disassemble it. The grace of a victor. Midway between power and gentility, the decorated parchment paper that served as a home to the burger crumpled, tilting vertically so it could get closer to his mouth. Then, in a single well-timed blow, he took a bite. A bite that aimed to eat and taste it all. A corner of the beef patty, a bite of onions, a dab of mayo, a bit of lettuce, a slice of the pickle, a sliver of the tomato. To squeeze out all the flavors at once.

Funny. For several years now I have come to terms with his way, his worldview. For several years, whether I liked it or not, he had been etching on me how he wanted things to be. Not what I wanted. I was still in high school, but with one bite of a burger my new business insight came into the world. In fact, I had already drawn this conclusion from politics, from the world, from history. But here it just got sharper, seared on the hot, greasy grill of my life. Every deal must have many elements. Components of different strengths and textures. Some you can compromise on and some you can't. Some that only you know how to deliver and others can't do without. Some you can swallow bitterly, and others that are the very reason you're making the deal in the first place.

Every deal begins with parts that must somehow be split, cut, added to, clumped together and wrapped up. Like here, Joey, the expert flipper, starts by cleanly slashing through the bun with a cutting knife. Ripping apart its virginity, showing it how cruel life can be. He then flops the slices on the grill to brand them forever, in a harsh rite of passage. I also reached with my hands, which are much smaller than my dad's, and gave it my best try. At first I touched the paper wrapper with some trepidation. I wondered if I'd be up to the task of grabbing all of it without dropping anything. Of keeping all the components together without squishing them too much. I imitated him to the best of my ability.

   My coming-of-age ritual focused completely around holding that bun. I turned it straight up like a ballet dancer, brought it up closer, opened my mouth to the point of pain, and narrowed the space between my lips and teeth while pushing my slightly slanted head forward into the giant burger my hands held out to me. Hands that were trying to preserve the existing. I took the biggest bite I could put in my mouth, with tabasco, cheese, onion rings, lettuce, bacon. With each component I liked it more and less. I made every effort to suppress the tears in my eyes from the spiciness, the pain in my tongue from the burning patty, the taste I disliked most—the taste of pickled cucumbers. A man who takes the whole deal without flinching. All I could do was show him there was nothing unusual here, that I was actually in the habit of eating like this. That I wasn't having a whole giant burger with everything on it for the first time—but rather for the millionth time.

   Just then. Only then, after I had finished chewing most of the bite, did I offer Dad my deal.

"If I get a car, you can give me larger, heavier goods to move around. Things that are important to you, which you can entrust only to me. Things you won't let others deliver. I can also drive farther away. So we both get something out of it, not just me," I said like a grown-up. "So we've got goods that can travel greater distances. We've got me, who you can trust. We've got the politics of the elections. There's also everything I already help out with—designing promotional leaflets for people's mailboxes, ideas to reach new audiences. I promise you I will read everything I need to know about politics. I promise I will sit with you and Mom to brainstorm on new initiatives. Anything you want. I will keep doing everything and much more. But let me go on reading."

Dad listened. Took another bite. The fan rattled, hummed. People came and went. "Get me a giant burger without the fries. And two servings of onion rings." Dad went on, taking a bite, another bite, and another, until I thought my idea might collapse. Because with him there was no silence of the vanquished. On the contrary. His silence always implied one must prepare oneself for an atom bomb to be dropped.

"I'm your man, Dad," I said, trying to reinforce the walls of the fortress I had built. Maybe he was mentally kicking me down the stairs already.

Only about halfway through the meal, Dad wiped some leftover ketchup off his chin with a napkin and said: "Fine." After a short pause he continued, "I'm going to perfect your idea. There might be something you can do for me. I thought you were a little too young for that, but apparently you're not. This will go well with your reading."

Dad asked me to deliver things. Not heavy packages, but rather small bags. Each time to a different place. Places I had to drive to. Gas stations, restaurants, cafes. When we were done eating, he explained to me how I would accidentally run into people there. They would drop something. And so would I. I'd have to practice doing so and keep it a secret. A secret between men that is hidden between double burger patties. Once they drop the item, I pick it up and return it to them, adding something that I will pass on without anyone noticing.

And how does reading history and philosophy books fit the scheme? It fits perfectly. Who would suspect a skinny kid in jeans and glasses, with hair that's a little long, reading Nietzsche in a café over a glass of soda?

I left the hamburger place feeling tremendously excited with my achievement. And also crowned in glory by my own self. After all, it is a well-known fact that spies discuss top-secret missions only in crowded cafés. They look less suspicious and there is a lot of background noise. I was convinced that Dad was doing something for the security of the country. Especially after he told me that this should be kept strictly between the two of us.

I made the deliveries for years. I did so dutifully, like a faithful dog. I did not pull out of our arrangement. Eventually I reduced the number of deliveries because of the pressure of my college studies and the hours I devoted to writing papers. I didn't consider that a big deal. I didn't think it might be a problem. I assumed Dad realized this and was giving me a break. I didn't know he was just shriveling away, not feeling well, that his health was deteriorating. I did not inquire about his illnesses, and I wasn't aware he could no longer control me because he himself was no longer very much in control.

Only once was our arrangement put to the test. It almost ended. It was when I was in the military. Dina, a biology student at the university, a few years older than me, worked at the store in the north of town. Dina, who dreamed of working in a bookstore but settled for a candy and game store. And me, whom my dad got, following grueling months of basic training, an exemption so I could be closer to home, and a special permission to work in the family business. "To help support the family," as was written in the third form we filled out.

I tried to be at the north-end branch as often as possible when Dina was there. It started with small exchanges, short conversations, and concise text messages. Visiting the store was a chance to get a quick look at her skillful movements behind the checkout counter, to listen to a snippet of her conversation with the customers, to the way she asked other employees questions showing genuine interest in her tone of voice, loud and feminine but not indulgent or condescending.

One day I brought an urgent package to the branch and stayed on to read in the air conditioned venue. I delved into a book I had in the car. "What are you reading?" she asked. We both gazed into each other's eyes. This was a starting point that, with surprising speed, was honed into a sophisticated machine that knew how to jump from one language to another based on the timing. The language of the heart and soul was spoken under the auspices of noon dreariness, since no one set foot inside the store at that hour. It was a conversation with three voices—hers, mine and the whir of the air conditioner. If, by chance, a customer or supplier happened to enter the store, the terminology was deftly changed to subjects like inventories and crates, cash balances and average tickets.

So it went. Only a few minutes each time. Maybe fifteen minutes, no more. Each time I discovered something new: the crease in the corner of her lips when she said my name, the look of pleasant surprise when she saw me, her hand squeezing mine, and then holding it again for a little longer. The touch that turned from accidental to deliberate. And then, into a hug when I embraced her in the warehouse behind the store.

I arrived for different reasons every time, and tried to back them up with some relevant activity. I returned with conclusions, proposals for expanding the branch and numerous plans. I suggested Dina replace the manager. I pointed out she was a dedicated employee. I prepared an action plan to double the store's sales. It wasn't just my plan, it was our plan. We worked on it together for two months. Two months during which the chambers of my heart fluttered with joy every time I knew I had a thought to share with her. Two months in which I watched her intently read the next draft of the plan. Study it.

When she was concentrating hard, there was a slight wheezing in her breath, like a light whistle. When she lifted her head from the page, she always waited a moment before saying anything. It always started on a positive note, then wandered from a comment on an idea that dealt with the core of the plan to an insight of its margins, and back again. She concluded by summing up the combination of all her comments, as if in her analysis she were drawing a mandala.

One day I asked to go to the branch. My excuse was that

I wanted to do a spot-check of the cash register closure and the monthly revenues. To see if our plan was working. Dad looked pleased. I got there in the evening. We sat outside. We drank beer from plastic cups. We laughed at the stupidest things. Her head rested on my shoulder for a moment, mine rested on her here and there. It was a year in which my world blossomed and fell into place. A year when everything seemed to me to be in order, right and logical. I was my father's hope. I helped him out. He was happy with me. A year in which I myself did not understand why I woke up every morning with a smile, looking forward to the rest of the week.

Until he caught me. One day he led me to the kitchenette and opened the door of a large pantry that contained several screens. He pressed some buttons on the control panel, and the screen showed Dina and me laughing, cuddling and kissing.

I was twenty years old. An adult. I obviously had my merits but, in practice, I had been naive and was completely at my dad's mercy. He taught me how bad it is for a man to go chasing after what's bothering him. He had already talked to me about it in the past. I tried to argue, to say that it happened by chance and wouldn't be repeated. But every statement came out of my mouth muddled. Dad had no mercy. He demanded I stop it immediately, and threatened to assign someone to ride in the car with me at all times.

"If I can't trust you, there's no deal. No life. No continuity. All is lost." He said this without batting an eyelid. In a moment of distress I wanted to propose serving him Dina on a silver platter, sacrificing her so that she would no longer be an employee. But Dad made it clear that it wasn't just the relationship between a boss and his subordinate. It was about relationships in general.

I was seething. I was beside myself. I paced back and forth in the small kitchenette, to the office and back to the screens. "I'm a man. I am an adult. You said it yourself. Let me make my own choices," I said, biting into my imaginary giant burger as hard as I could. With the tabasco, the onions, the pickles and the lettuce, and everything that made my mouth ache.

"What choices? You can't choose. I choose for you, because I know. You know things. You have talents—I know how to make use of them," he said, making an indisputable statement.

The rage bubbling up in me choked me until it erupted. "I love her and she loves me. Do you understand, Dad? We love each other," I said it like it was Martin Luther King's *I Have a Dream* speech. My whole body stood there at that moment, as if I were creating the world, as if I were opening everyone's eyes with the gospel. Speaking like Jesus to the multitudes. Using grave words in an attempt to convince Dad that Dina was great for me. That we had a good connection and a common language. Not only good for me but for the business too. That we could maybe even bring her in as a partner.

But Dad seemed to be just waiting for me to utter those sentences. As if he knew my magazine was full of those bullets even before I fired them. "Love? Bullshit. You just have to fuck. That's all. Get rid of it and be done."

My dad always spoke decisively, he was always sharp. But I had never heard him say the word fuck, and certainly not the word love. I had painstakingly ground and placed on a sizzling grill the patties I stuffed into a bun to serve dad—a prized dish in his feast of victory, which he would eat with the grace of the victor. He, however, squashed it into a hockey puck and smashed me to bits in an instant.

"Do you remember that summer? Do you? The summer when I told you that if you needed it, you should come to me? Then come to me," he said. He then repeated it louder. "Come to me, because I have the solution for you."

With my last vestiges of control, I agreed to keep my end of the bargain with the deliveries, on the condition that he would let me continue my philosophy studies at the university and get my degree. I knew he needed me as much as I needed him but that I couldn't be with Dina. I crossed a line, in his eyes, and he insisted on getting me back. POW's are never left behind.

I cried that night but, in the morning, I woke up like a robot. Time and my father's power did the job. A few days later he took me to a house with several women. All the way there he gave me strict instructions, as if preparing me to audition for a role in a play. "Don't worry, I know her well. She's doing it as a special favor for me."

When we arrived, he opened the car door and directed me to one of the apartments in an old building with several floors. I went up stubborn stairs that were far apart. I knocked on the door and said Dad's name. I was let in by someone wearing a very short green dress, spaghetti-thin straps and high heels. Lipstick. Hair tied back. I said Dad's name again, as he told me to.

The smell of her bedroom was thick and sweet to the point of nausea. A purple light shone dimly. "Even if you feel like it," Dad had coached me, "don't kiss her. It does no good." I asked anyway. Just a kiss or two. Nothing more. "Whatever you want," she said. I pressed my lips to hers. I put my arms behind her back. I tightened them a little and concentrated on the touch. I tried in vain to convert the bath-sponge feel of her lips into something else.

Then she took off the green dress in one easy movement and revealed thin dark panties. I did the same. I took off my pants. I hugged her again. Her gaze shifted to the side. I still tried to stroke her. I reached back trying to get her to stroke me. "Can you caress me?" I asked in a whisper, almost begging. Her hands moved coldly up and down me, like a service elevator controlled by the buttons pressed by its users.

A few seconds later she took off my briefs in a skillful motion. Then she began rubbing her hands against my limbs. She operated and activated forces that cannot be turned back. She increased the speed of the train so I couldn't stop. Sorrow was perhaps replaced by rage, or perhaps by frustration. I held on with my hands to her thin panties. Inadvertently I pulled them with so much force that they came off and tore. She stepped backwards, unfazed by any of my movements. Experienced. She let her body fall back on the bed and my body hold hers. She only barely stopped me for a moment to put on a condom that was already on the bed. She did it in seconds, prepared for this scenario. And I, who was not in control of anything in this scene, tore my clothed cock from her hands, violently. I leaned my body against her, ramming in, storming inside.

I relieved myself like someone committing suicide. Ideologically right but defeated. Too violent and extreme, and having to pay a heavy personal price. I now wanted to get a comforting rest at her place, and maybe rest in eternal peace. To caress, to ease the tension. Maybe even cry.

But my dad warned me. Don't do it. It's wrong. I didn't move. I lay on top of her consumed by guilt. Asking myself if he wasn't actually right, in the end. That it all happened just because I needed this.

Dad knew what the cure was for the feelings I still had for Dina. A few more times of sending me there, instructing me on more new methods of unloading my baggage and getting rid of the disturbing memory of the girl I liked, brushed away from me questions about what I felt towards her or what I feel in general.

One time, some men knocked on the door while I was there. She put her hand on my mouth and asked me not to say anything, not to move. I closed my eyes and didn't move. I was strong. I hugged her. She stroked me softly. Until the men left. I felt her fear uniting our bodies. I felt what a relaxed, serene, loving body feels like. She asked me what my name was for the first time, and I asked her. I told her about my love for philosophy. It made her laugh. She saw I was shaking. She gave me water and a soda, and said to tell my dad that, on that day, I didn't have to pay her. That was when I started to feel something. Something that might have been the thing Dad warned me about. And I didn't go back there.

That's how my father used to steamroll roads on the blazing tar I poured before him. He ran me over with the heavy machinery, pinning me onto the road that was getting cooler, over which people and cars would soon be walking and driving, without feeling a thing.

* * *

I left the kitchenette in the main office and returned to my mom. She had fixed her hair in the meantime. She rearranged her dress. Reapplied her make-up. "The Pick-up Sticks, Go Fish and Scattergories," she said without me asking her while she sipped her coffee. "It's because you stopped with your errands. That's the reason."

I knew about politics, I knew how Kennedy was assassinated. I knew about the Trojan War, about existentialism. But I didn't know what it was that I used to do. It is possible to be a political consultant, one who can see complexities, an expert in games of chess between crooks, and also completely innocent at the same time. It is possible to not connect the dots when they complete your own blindness to yourself.

Chapter 23

It's morning at my Airbnb apartment, not far from the Tenerife airport. I pack the last of my belongings, go out to the lobby, and sit outside until my taxi arrives.

It's early and there's no one on the street. Only the light of dawn. Some birds. I walk back and forth in the slight chilliness that's warming up. Then, out of nowhere, two pairs of arms grab me hard from behind. I'm blindfolded. My heart jumps to the sky. On my last day? Am I going to be robbed on the last morning of my stay here?

I don't try to resist. I do my best to go along. I bend and flex against their strong grip so as not to get hurt or break anything. Trying to gain a few more seconds of rational thinking about the last thing I would have thought of.

"Give me all your cash," shouts one of them. "Give us all your cash, tourist. Where is it?"

I'm scared of being beaten up or maybe even shot. Afraid of ending this whole journey dead or with some crippling injury.

"I don't keep any cash on me," I shout out in English several times. I fight the tremor in my voice so I don't come through as weak. "I hardly have any. I've bought everything here on Google Pay." My body refuses to listen to me. With great difficulty I manage to reach into my pocket and pull out my wallet. I hand them a few hundred-dollar bills.

They laugh. They let go of me for a moment, but still hold me by the hem of my clothes. "So you've got Google Pay," says one of them in a voice that sounds a bit circus-y. Modern bandits, I think to myself. They tighten the blindfold and lead me for a few yards around the corner. Probably no more than a block or two.

They seat me on a chair in what I imagine to be a shop or a warehouse. One of them pulls my cell phone out of his pocket and forcefully leads my hand to an ATM on which he types some numbers. I feel the haptic vibration that follows an approved transaction. Another one and yet another one. "Hey," he shouts. "Five thousand dollars. He's maxed out on both credit cards. I've scraped all I could." And someone answers him: "I see. I'm on my way."

I manage to peek a little out of the corner of my eye. The place looks familiar to me, but it's still hard for me to recognize it through the narrow slit. Now they are taking off my blindfold. Only one of them remains here, gripping my arm tightly. "Just let me go. I have a flight to catch. There's no way I'll file a report," I say, trying to sound calm and confident like I've done in all those crisis management situations.

"Of course you won't complain about us," shouts someone from behind. Now I see the place, recognize the voice and put everything together. All the questions about my condition and the excessive kindness. She was the one who recommended this B&B to me. So simple and stupid. "Of course you won't file a complaint about us," this time she is right behind me. Clara expresses her disappointment in the fact that her instincts misled her. That a fifty-year-old man approached her, wearing fine walking shoes, using mostly Google Pay, and appeared to own a good car and one or two real estate properties. How could she have been wrong and thought he could afford a house that cost a million or more?

Clara reverts to her European manners and demands remittance for the offense she suffered. "I hope you don't mind that I also added to my commission some of the outlays we had on your account. You'd better leave now."

Chapter 24

Deal

Contrary to what the police believed twenty years ago, the criminals were not targeting the prostitutes and pimps in our neighbor's building. They were after us. The names of the games were a cover for the money received in exchange for my delivery jobs.

A week later my mother received the fat guy and the bearded partner in our home. I saw the movement of her right hand on the hand of one of them, and her left hand touching his shoulder for a moment. The kiss with a slight tilt to the left of the face and the puckering of the lips towards his cheek. Her body leaning forward a little and showing excessive affection. I studied her inquisitive "Hmm," the slight nod of the head. When her hair was gathered, she would shake it.

I wasn't too interested in the details of selling the business, even though Mom insisted on involving me in the deal. She used all her artfulness—the fake interest, the artificial hug—and closed the deal. Criminals no longer harassed us. Handling of the matter was transferred to the partners as part of their acquisition of our share of the company.

There was no Dad to exercise his talent as a merchant. There was no lever to operate. We were helpless and under threat. My mom did her best and the partners bought us out at a price my dad would never have agreed to.

I only made one deal with Mom. I asked her to help me find a job in the capital. A few weeks later I was interviewed at the first advertising agency in the big city that wished to hire me. The firm where I rose to the position of VP. The firm from which I was recruited into the partnership. With the death of the Department of Foreign Affairs of the Jonah chain of stores, Mom commanded me to live in the capital.

Three years after I started working there, I was summoned to a room which I knew as being empty, unutilized. It was the senior partner's office. She spent very little time there, and mostly after work hours. She was busy with other matters.

When I opened the door, I saw the young woman from the funeral. I already considered myself a veteran in eating burgers with lots of toppings. I had become indifferent to tabasco and pickles. I was task-oriented. Suave. I was also good at my job and knew I had something to sell. Admittedly not philosophy. That was not useful and, while we're at it—a soul is not a useful thing. Neither is love. Assuming there is such a thing at all. But I was a successful copywriter, I saw the complexities and provided insights that were immediately useful to anyone holding office. My managers saw it right away.

My mom, by the way, did everything she could to keep the Department of Foreign Affairs alive. She got up every day, showered, chose a nice dress and went wandering around the offices of NGO directors, lawyers and mayors.

But without an active business and without significant financial resources, her office was devoid of any purpose. The visits became increasingly rare.

Even when she tried to run for the position of Chairperson of the City Volunteering Center—she failed in her efforts. A few months later, she secluded herself at home and remained there until she died. Few came to her funeral. I complied with the required minimum and immediately returned to the capital.

The young woman from the funeral, hereafter the Senior Partner, ended a conversation with me about performance, career and salary increases that everyone wants in their burgers. I was about to get up. "I have something to tell you," she said, stopping me, "I knew your father much better than you think." I sat there in silence. Dressed in my emotionally bulletproof suit. Nothing could shake me right at that moment. Nothing.

"I see." I put two and two together myself, following in Dad's footsteps. "And did my mother know?" I asked cooly. Without any drama. Bearing in mind that every dish is made with many ingredients, and you only need to identify them, see what the other party needs and likes, and what they don't.

"Your mother knew. That was the deal between them. You know how your father loved deals."

"I see," I repeated.

I reached with both hands for the burger that lay on its side with its mouth open, having almost passed out, loaded with all the goodies: lucrative projects, customers who sang my praises. I placed my hands on the tray, and tightened my grip on its sides. I saw her vulnerability.

"OK. Why are you telling me this? After all, neither

my mom nor my dad are alive." I clamp firmly so as to contain, but not to break, not to disassemble. Deft as a maestro. Midway between power and gentility, the decorated parchment paper that served as a home to the burger crumpled, tilting vertically so it could get closer to my mouth.

"I didn't want it to be weird between us, from my side," she said to me. I was convinced I saw moisture in her eyes. "I wanted to get it off my chest. It's just between the two of us. Don't worry. I haven't told anyone."

Then, in a single well-timed blow, I took a bite. A bite that aimed to eat and taste it all. A corner of the beef patty, a bite of onions, a dab of mayo, a bit of lettuce, a slice of the pickle, a sliver of the tomato. To squeeze out all the flavors at once. To savor the moment in its entirety.

"I want to be Vice President," I said. "I deserve it."

She gave me the job. As a shrewd businesswoman, she saved for herself an unexpected victory on another front. "Your father loved you," she said to me. Her mouth was slightly open, her eyes piercing, the half circle of her eyelashes was long and curled upwards like wings. Her chin rested on her wrists in a triangle with her elbows resting on the black desk.

The air-conditioned office. The bright curtains. The dark table. The TV in the background. The executive desk toys. The metal chairs. The low-pile carpet. The office door that doesn't flatter. The impartial neon lights.

Chapter 25

I do my best not to soil the couch while eating my dinner. Right in front of me, about seven feet away, is the trio. A large window almost from the floor up to its head in the sky, framing a glimpse of the desert. Beige hills adorned with small stones and hard rocks. In the distance, the state border. To the left of the window, a flat monitor, hanging from a muscular, metallic arm mounted on the wall, and way to the left is an oil painting on canvas in daring colors that could well be a wild hairdo, or perhaps minced ideas being squeezed out of a grinder. About three by six feet.

I write a lot. *Schreiben macht frei*—writing sets you free. But it only really sets you free if it has imprisoned you in a concentration camp. Because when you write yourself down, truly yourself, everyone sees you. And, when that happens, you might sometimes think that dying would be the better option.

That's why I sometimes replace writing with drawing. The canvas endures everything. It engulfs portions of color, it absorbs rage. It routes out decisions in red, yellow, green. Color that's thick or thin, smeared or hilly. Colors that reveal but also conceal well among layers of pigments.

A year after the trip, my right arm still hurts once in a while, a souvenir from the hoodlum in Tenerife.

The other room in the house contains an easel, heaps of paint tubes, a plate or two. One of the room's walls is a mural depicting a forest of wonders with tall thin trees and stairs made of tree trunks. A painting of houses standing on the steep slope of a mountain, near the sea, and huge black rocks hangs on another wall.

Every evening, after the shower and just before dinner, it lies there waiting for me. Charging with renewed energy at the outlet. I place my hand gently around the curved edges of its dark body. A leg buried in a transparent plastic shelf entwining four silver snail coils that rotate within and among themselves, taking turns, in circular motions. Each of them encases a whole world of small parts designed to perform a smooth, almost imperceptible task. Like the caress of a hand.

I turn on the shaver. A machine that arrived one day for young Lake, not for a ceremony celebrating his manhood, but to shave his head for the treatments. The failed treatments. And so it came to pass that the machine shaved off Lake's hair, inch by inch, while the years of his future were hacked off all at once.

Every other day for six months my hand gently caressed the scalp with the light emerging stubble. I was brought back for a moment to the yellow fluff I used to stroke when he was a two-week-old baby at the home for abandoned babies. I hoarded up a stash of warmth like a rechargeable battery, the opportunity to caress him while shaving his forehead. The shaver glided over the hemisphere that held some of his personality. My hand on his shoulder brushing aside a strand of hair was actually patting it. I did a cheek, but actually I was embracing. I went over the sideburns, kissing. And he gave me of himself. He relaxed and let go.

Now I shave with it and, every evening, Lake shaves in me. The silver wheels that crisscrossed his head hundreds of times now burn my cheeks, promising to leave me smooth. We caress each other through the shaver, my Lake and me, and it's simultaneously pleasant and painful. After the night, in the morning, he launches himself like a satellite to orbit my moon.

I pause the audio book I'm listening to during dinner, to air out a bit. I turn on the TV. "And this evening it was revealed that a gang of smugglers was caught after an investigation that lasted over two years," says the anchorman. "At the press conference he held, the Police Commissioner displayed hundreds of vinyl records that had been seized after the smugglers used a surprising method. Capsules of rare, banned narcotics were hidden inside newly stamped records. In order to lure them into delivering the records to other countries, seventeen and eighteen-year-olds were offered paid, low-cost trips abroad, and given rare records as well as tickets to live concerts. The young traffickers were unaware of the dangerous substances hidden in the records they carried. Clinical experts estimate that each capsule is worth thousands of dollars, since these are difficult-to-obtain substances used in complex formulas that sell for tens of thousands of dollars, as part of the preparation process of drugs to treat rare diseases."

In the background are journalists standing outside the house of a tall, elegant lady with a slight foreign accent, and her assistant. She speaks briefly. Most of the job is done by the man next to them, the one who responds to the reporters with confidence and in an eloquent language. That's my partner.

Or, to be more precise, my former partner.

Acknowledgments

Dan Toren, Efrat Gosh, Yoram Mokedi, Itamar Shafrir, Hana Volknir, Eefje de Visser and Roni Gelbfisch.